Waiting on Summer

COLLAR & CUFFS BOOK ONE

BELLA SETTARRA

Second Electronic Publication: Bella Settarra Publishing - February 2020

First Printed Publication: Bella Settarra Publishing - March 2016

Second Printed Publication: Bella Settarra Publishing - July 2022

Dedication

To Jo. Thank you for all your support. You'll never know how much it means to me.

GLOSSARY OF WAITING ON AND KITCHEN TERMS

This is a list of some of the terminology used in the *Collar and Cuffs* series. Some terms may differ between establishments and/or countries.

Waiting on—the term used for serving customers in a restaurant.

Silver Service—the practice of serving each item of food separately using a fork and spoon (occasionally two forks or two spoons depending on food). Term refers to the use of silverware—food is served from silver platters/dishes with silver cutlery.

Plate Service—the act of serving meals already plated, usually used in cafés, diners etc.

Dumbwaiter—type of sideboard that is assigned to each station to hold cutlery, cloths, etc.

Station—the area or tables to which a specific waiter/waitress is assigned to serve.

Covers—the number of guests eating, i.e. "set that table for six covers," or "we served over two hundred covers tonight."

Deuce—refers to a table of two diners or a party of two.

Busboy/busgirl/busperson—a member of the restaurant staff who is assigned to help the waiting on staff by clearing and setting tables, taking dirty dishes from the restaurant to the dishwasher, etc. (In Britain this person is usually referred to as a commis waiter.)

Bussing—roles performed by a busboy.

Front of house—the area of the restaurant that a customer will usually see.

Back of house—any area of a restaurant that a customer won't be able to see, usually refers to the kitchen, but can also include changing rooms, utility areas, etc.

The line—the area of the kitchen where waiting on staff wait to receive their food orders. (Sometimes used as in "waiting in line," "waiting on the line," etc.)

The window—the area of the kitchen where waiting on staff are passed their food orders. "The line" leads up to this section.

Expeditor (or "expo")—this person is responsible for overseeing the food leaving the kitchen to be taken to the restaurant. They usually stand by "the window" to monitor quality, speed, etc.

Eighty-six/Eight-six—refers to an item that is "off" the menu, or a customer who is being or has been refused service.

"In the weeds"—hellishly busy.

Slammed—not quite "in the weeds" but close to it.

Jumpin—very busy.

"On the fly"—done straight away, i.e. a VIP's meal may be done "on the fly" so he doesn't have to wait around for it.

To walk—to literally walk out of the job; to leave before the end of the shift.

Chapter One

S ummer paused outside the building in surprise. When she had answered the advert for waiting on staff in a high-class restaurant, this was not quite what she expected.

Although it looked like a neat, two-story building in a nice part of the city, it wasn't exactly high profile.

There didn't seem to be any stores around this area, and the few office blocks she noticed on the way seemed to be quiet places, maybe full of old men studying dusty ledgers—certainly not the kind of places that would provide a steady clientele to an expensive restaurant and club.

A black, shiny sign stood above the large double doors of the white brick building. "Collar and Cuffs" was written in bold, but not brash, letters. It showed the neck of a man on one side with a white collar and a black bow tie, and on the other end of the sign was a pair of masculine hands showing shirt cuffs fastened with gold cuff links.

It certainly looked like a classy place.

She watched a cab pull up, delivering a couple of men dressed in expensive-looking suits, and she followed them into the large reception area.

As she did so she was aware of someone walking in behind her, and she turned to see a gorgeous guy in a gray suit smiling down at her. Big brown eyes met her green ones, and he gave her a wicked smile, cocking one eyebrow as if surprised to see her.

"Hi. I haven't seen you here before." His voice was like soft velvet, smooth and deep.

"No... er... I've come to see Mr. Ray about a new position," she stammered.

His salacious grin told her that she had phrased that all wrong, and she blushed at the innuendo.

"A new position, eh? Well, good luck with that, sugar. And if it doesn't work out with him perhaps you'd like to try a new position under me instead? I'll see you around."

He winked at her, and his eyes twinkled cheekily. Summer found herself staring at him as he took off in the direction of a corridor.

Hoping to see him again, she cleared her throat and her thoughts before approaching the large counter facing her.

"Summer Marsden," she told the lady behind the

desk. "I'm here to meet Dominic Ray about the waiting on position."

The young girl smiled at her and told her to take a seat. She looked very elegant in a black shift dress with a white jacket, echoing the monochrome theme of the building. Her hair was neatly tied in a ponytail, and she wore large glasses on her pretty face.

Summer sat on a large sofa, which lined one wall of the foyer, and took the opportunity to study the area.

It looked very modern with streamlined furniture, broken up a little by bright green foliage, which may or may not have been artificial. Summer was just contemplating touching one of the lush leaves of a nearby parlor palm to check its authenticity when she heard someone clear their throat from the front desk.

"Miss Marsden?"

She looked up and felt herself flush at the sight of the handsome man in a morning suit who stood completely upright with his chin up and his hand outstretched to greet her.

"Um...yes, that's me."

She stood up, trembling slightly as she clutched her folder and purse, almost dropping them both in her hurry to get over to him. She held out her hand and was sure she saw a flicker of a smile from him over her quaking.

"Dominic Ray, the maître d'hôtel. Welcome to Collar and Cuffs."

His voice was deep and confident, with a slightly

British accent, and Summer couldn't work out why she felt so intimidated by him.

He was very good-looking and had quite an austere manner, complemented by his short, dark hair and very dark eyes. He was completely clean-shaven and looked the epitome of an upper-class English gentleman. His hand was cool and his hold was firm as he shook her hot, trembling hand in his.

"Thank you," she mumbled nervously.

She followed him through to the back of the reception area and into a very large, plush restaurant. Her feet sank into the thick carpet, and she noticed the pristine white tablecloths, which almost shone under the light of the overhead chandeliers. The whole place boasted an opulence and class that made her gasp.

"Take a seat."

He led her over to a table by the window, which hadn't yet been laid up for dinner, and she almost submerged into the soft leather of the chair.

"Your résumé was quite impressive," he began, opening a leather portfolio on the table in front of him. "You have brought your certificates, I assume?" He was staring at the plastic folder in her sweaty hand.

"Yes," she said, hastily opening the cover.

"That's all right. HR will check them afterwards," he told her, putting up his hand to halt her movements.

"Oh right. Of course." Why on earth would he deal with anything so menial? She secretly admonished herself for even considering such a ridiculous notion.

"You are qualified and experienced in silver service waiting on," he continued, "and have extensive knowledge of serving alcoholic beverages."

Summer nodded, not surprised at his precise use of terminology. No "waiting staff" or "servers" here. She grinned as she imagined his expression if she were to urge the customers to "have a nice day." Then she realized that they were probably called "clients" or "patrons" around here anyhow.

Dominic cleared his throat, and she suddenly noticed he was staring at her. With a flush of horror she also noted she had actually giggled out loud and was wearing a grin like a Cheshire cat! She quickly straightened in her seat, cleared her own throat, and composed herself as the familiar sensation of flaming-hot embarrassment swamped her face.

He looked back down at his papers, but she couldn't help noticing a tiny smirk twitch the corners of his lips.

"Have you ever worked in an establishment of this caliber before?"

She narrowed her eyes at him. He no doubt knew full well she had not.

"Not exactly like this, but I worked in some top London restaurants when I was over there," she replied, trying to sound impressive.

"Oh really?" He was slowly turning over the pages in front of him, obviously seeking evidence of her assertion. "Where was this? The Grosvenor House? The Ritz? The..."

"No, none of those," she interrupted quickly, envisaging him ringing up all those places to substantiate her claim. "I worked in some slightly smaller, *elite* places. Sort of...um...quintessential English tearooms and places like that," she clarified in a small voice.

"I see." He closed the folder, looking at her carefully. "But you have carried out full silver service?"

"Oh yes," she assured him, beaming. OK, so she may not have worked anywhere like this before—she'd never even *seen* anywhere like this before—but she knew how to hold a spoon and fork in one hand and balance a heavy platter on her forearm.

"Show me," he said abruptly, springing to his feet.

"W-what?" She stared at him.

"Show me. Get yourself some serving cutlery from that dumbwaiter and show me how you carry yourself. You can use one of those serving dishes." He pointed to a wooden sideboard at the serving station nearby and watched her expectantly.

Her heart thudded as she stood up and went to where he had waved his arm. She opened the drawer and took out a serving spoon and fork, being careful to polish them on a serving cloth neatly folded on the sparkling clean surface. She bent down to the cupboard beneath her and took up a two-portion serving dish, which she placed on the serving cloth in her left hand. She walked over to the table where Dominic had regained his seat and pretended to serve him something from the dish.

As she leaned into his left side she caught a waft of

his spicy aftershave and felt her stomach lurch in excitement. He really was an incredibly handsome man, and he had a very firm jaw, which added to his austere appearance. There was something very commanding in his manner.

"What is it?" His question cut into her thoughts like a knife through hot butter, and she quickly straightened up, wondering what she had done wrong.

"I-I'm sorry?" she mumbled as her mind scrambled for a coherent thought.

"What is it?" he asked again. His dark eyes blazed into hers, and she felt herself go hot right down to her core.

She just stared at him blankly.

He sighed. "What are you offering me?"

She suddenly wondered if he had read her thoughts about him.

"N-nothing," she stuttered. "I mean...I was just..." She felt herself blush from the roots of her hair down to her toenails as she struggled for the right words. She bit her lip and took a step backward.

Dominic frowned. He took another deep breath before speaking.

"When you offer the guest some food, do you not clarify what it is so that they can make an informed choice about whether or not to accept?"

Summer let out a nervous little laugh.

"Oh yes, of course." She relaxed and went back to her position, but he was already glancing at his Rolex.

"We haven't got time to continue now. The staff will be arriving soon. Just remember to ask in future—oh, and the serving dish should have been placed on a salver before being presented to the guest."

He got up quickly, and Summer rushed to put the cutlery and dish back.

"Those will need to be washed," he told her.

She felt herself blush again.

"Oh yes... of course... I'm sorry, I..."

"Leave them on the top for now." He waved an irritated arm at her. "You need to get up to HR with your paperwork. I've signed the induction form for you, but you might need a little more practice. We'll see how you do tonight."

Summer gasped. Tonight? "I've got the job?" she asked excitedly.

"If you do well tonight." His face didn't even crack a smile. "You need to take these up to HR. Through reception. Take the elevator to the next floor. You'll have to wait there while they verify everything and take your details. They'll also give you a uniform and show you where your locker is. Get changed and come back here as soon as you can. Service begins at seven o'clock sharp."

Summer took the portfolio from him and picked up her folder and purse.

"Yes, I will. Thank you, thank you so much."

She scurried out of the restaurant and over toward reception.

"Hold on," a voice shouted as the doors began to

close in front of her. She quickly pressed the button to hold the elevator as another very good-looking man ran over.

"Thanks," he said with a grin as he got in beside her. "Which way?" He was standing next to the keypad. He too smelled of expensive aftershave, and he was dressed in black trousers and a smart green shirt. His fair hair shone under the fluorescent lighting, and he had gorgeous blue eyes.

"HR. Up, I think," she said, noticing there were three floors to the building, not just two as she had thought.

"Up it is," he said with a delightful smile as he keyed in the upper floor. "I'm Brad, by the way. Brad Dexter." He held out his hand, and she shook it.

"Summer Marsden."

She smiled back at him. It was nice to meet someone friendly after the intensity of her new boss. This guy was real good-looking too, though not quite as handsome as the man in the foyer earlier.

"Fancy a drink later, Summer?"

"Um... I... er..." She felt that blush coming back on.

"Go on. I'd like to get to know you, and this elevator doesn't have a lot going for it in terms of meeting places," he said with a wink.

Summer giggled. "OK. I'd like that."

"Great. I'll be in the Bottom Bar later. Just come find me when you're free." With that the elevator stopped, and they both got out.

"Well, I guess I'll see you later, Brad," she said with a smile. He seemed real amicable, and it would be nice to get to know some of the folks around here.

"Sure thing, sweetheart." Brad winked again as he made his way toward a corridor, while Summer headed for a small reception desk in front of her.

The receptionist was certainly friendly and pointed her toward the HR office where a very nice lady called Mandy sorted out her paperwork.

"I'll show you to your locker," she said after a few minutes and took Summer down another corridor to a large changing room.

"This is your key. Don't lose it or you'll have to pay for a replacement," Mandy told her with a smile. "Most girls put them on a chain around their necks, although there is a pocket in your skirt. What size are you?"

Summer hesitated before she told Mandy, a little self-conscious of her slightly curvaceous figure. Mandy unlocked a large cupboard and took out several items of clothing, including a pair of black high-heeled shoes.

"I know it's not the norm, but this is Collar and Cuffs—not much is normal here!" Mandy sniggered, no doubt from the look of shock on Summer's face.

"Well, OK." Summer grinned and started to change as Mandy left her.

The blouse was cut a little lower than she expected, with a pretty frill leading down the cleavage, and she had never been allowed to wear such a short skirt as part of her uniform before.

She was surprised to have even been issued black thigh highs to go with the outfit, and she admired herself in the mirror as she quickly combed her short hair and touched up her lip gloss.

As she stared at her reflection with the frilly blouse and short black skirt and heels, she thought how she looked more like she was going out to *eat* a meal, not serve one.

She smiled at her new look. With her short, pixie-cut hair and her natural makeup, no one would recognize her here. She took the tiny key and popped it onto her neck chain, which also held a small cross, and hurried off for work.

Summer was overwhelmed. The turnover rate was exhausting, with every table used at least three times during service, and she was surprised they didn't use a busboy to clear and set.

About halfway through the evening Summer entered the kitchen to join the line and was surprised to find that the back of house was in the weeds.

Although every member of staff was hurrying, and the expeditor was calling orders left, right, and center, there was a professional order about the place. There was no panic or rushing, and everyone was efficiently getting on with their jobs in an orderly manner, albeit fast.

"Table fourteen entrées, please," Summer told the expeditor when he turned to her.

Above the shouts all around the kitchen she could hear her order being called away, and soon food was being passed across the line to her.

"Eighty-six on filet mignon," the expeditor shouted over to her as she left the kitchen.

Damn! She'd sold a lot of the filet tonight, purposely pushing it as it was one of the most expensive dishes on the menu.

She served her guests, pleased her skills were improving as the night went on. It had been several years since she had actually used her silver service techniques—all of the cafés and diners she had found work in had used plate service, which was much easier, but she knew that tips were bound to be much higher in a place like this.

"Creamed potatoes?" Summer spoke loudly just as Dominic walked past her.

She was rewarded by a slight smirk from him. She smiled to herself. Dominic was a foreboding presence as he strutted around the restaurant, and she was sure he saw and heard everything that went on. She still felt very nervous whenever he came near or she caught him watching her from across the room. There was calmness in his demeanor though, which told her that no matter what happened in his domain he would be able to sort it out. The thought gave her confidence.

"Eighty-six on the chicken chasseur," Heaven told

her as she walked past with a platter of perfectly dressed salmon.

"Is it always like this?" Summer asked her quietly.

"Nope. Sometimes it gets busy." Heaven winked at her and grinned.

Summer giggled. Heaven Blake was a beautiful redhead with warm brown eyes that twinkled with mirth. She had been a tremendous help to Summer as they shared a station.

Heaven was a little older than the newbie, probably around thirty, Summer surmised, and had taken her under her wing somewhat.

Summer was eternally grateful for her help, especially as she was trying to convince their perfectionist maître d' she wasn't as stupid as he probably thought she was.

"He's not all that bad," Heaven whispered when they finally managed to take a breather by their dumbwaiter. She pinned a tendril of her wavy hair back into her beautiful chignon.

"Who?" Summer flushed, half wishing she still had her long, wavy locks.

"Master D." Heaven giggled as they both began to polish cutlery.

"Who?" Summer had asked the question before she remembered that, of course, "maître" meant "master." "Oh, him? He just makes me a bit nervous, that's all."

"He makes everyone nervous," Heaven confided. "It's just the way he is."

"It's not just the job then?"

"Nope. It's the man himself, I'm afraid." Heaven smiled. Summer wondered if she fancied the boss.

"Is he married?"

Heaven shook her head. "No, he's not married."

"Hmm. I think I can see why," Summer mused, fiddling with her service cloth.

"Do tell."

The deep voice in Summer's ear made her hair stand on end, and she felt every inch of her body glow boiling hot. She jumped around and saw Dominic Ray standing right behind her with an expectant expression on his face.

"Um...what?" she spluttered.

"I'd be very interested to hear your view on why I'm not married, Miss Marsden. Do tell us." Dominic's voice was loud enough to be heard over the murmuring of polite conversation, and everyone turned to look at her.

Summer closed her eyes, hoping that when she opened them again all these people would be gone, and she would find herself lying in her bed at home, with all this nothing more than a bad dream.

Unfortunately, life—her life anyway—was never quite so easy, and when she finally opened her eyes again she was still in the middle of the crowded restaurant with everyone watching her in stony silence. *Oh shit!*

"Um...I only meant...well...what I was going to say was..." Her voice was feeble even to her own ears as she murmured and stuttered.

"Go on." Dominic was tenacious. His eyebrows were

raised in expectation and his handsome face as straight as any poker player.

Summer glanced over at Heaven who gave her a sympathetic smile.

Taking a deep breath she attempted an audible answer. "I simply meant that although you're..." She suddenly decided against flattery. Not that she didn't think he was handsome, as she was about to say he was, but because there was no way she could actually *tell* him what she thought of his looks. Besides that, a guy like him would already know how drop-dead gorgeous he was and didn't need her to stroke his ego.

"Yes?"

Summer pouted a little. How dare he? And on her first night at that, she thought ruefully. And probably last too. *Damn*, she needed this job.

"Scary." She blurted the word out, not daring to look him in the face. There was a silence, and she couldn't put off examining his expression any longer. She peered up at him to see that he looked totally astounded. As he stared at her, his manner shifted slightly, and his face relaxed into the most gorgeous smile Summer had ever seen in her life.

"You think I'm *scary*, Miss Marsden?"

Now she just felt stupid! She could hear titters and chuckles all around the room, and she still felt every eye boring into her. She was hot and flustered as well as agitated and annoyed.

"Yes, Mr. Ray. I think you're scary. And that's why I

think you are not married." She spoke through gritted teeth.

The whole restaurant erupted into fits of laughter, staff included, and Summer wanted the ground to just open up and swallow her whole.

She was surprised to see that Dominic Ray was laughing along with everyone else. Well, at least he'd remember her as the girl who gave him a laugh.

As the hilarity died down and the guests went back to their meals, he leaned over to her. This was it! She closed her eyes, cringing as she felt his hot breath in her ear and waited for those immortal but dreaded words.

"Table ten needs clearing, Miss Marsden."

It took a minute for the words to sink in. She narrowed her eyes. Probably wanted her to finish the shift, she surmised. They'd be short staffed if he threw her out now. She seethed, debating on whether or not to walk. She bit her lip. If she walked out now Heaven would have to finish her shift, and that would not be fair to poor Heaven. Also, she might as well get paid for this shift. It was almost over anyway.

Straightening her back, she put her nose in the air, her serving cloth over her arm, and set off toward table ten.

"Good for you, dear," a middle-aged woman whispered in her ear as she took her dish.

Summer felt herself blush. "Thank you," she whispered back discreetly.

"If you think he's scary you need to meet my master."

A young black-haired girl grinned across the table. The large man next to her placed his hand over the girl's.

"Don't worry, sugar, his bark's much worse than his bite," another of their party confided, making the other guests titter.

Mortified, Summer recognized the man as the hunk from the foyer. She hadn't noticed him before as he had his back to her, but now she could clearly see his handsome profile. Bile rose in her throat as she realized that he had just witnessed her embarrassing ordeal.

He tried to say something else to her, but Heaven rescued her by coming over and taking their coffee orders. Summer just hurriedly cleared their plates.

"Thank you so much for all your help tonight," Summer told her friend as they finished laying the last table.

"You're welcome. I hope we can work together again soon."

Summer frowned. "I wish!"

Now it was Heaven's turn to frown. "What do you mean?"

"I doubt I'll be here after tonight. You saw what happened. He's bound to fire me after that fiasco," Summer said gloomily.

Heaven laughed. "Of course he won't fire you! Don't worry. He does have a sense of humor, you know?"

She gave Summer a friendly tap on her arm. "You did great tonight. Don't you worry."

Summer was surprised but not convinced. She saw

everyone huddle together around Dominic and felt a heavy thud in her stomach. She nudged Heaven and pointed over to where the waiting on staff were flocking.

"Team debrief," Heaven explained. "We have one every night. We get to go home after this." She smiled and threw an arm around Summer's shoulder, leading her over.

Like a lamb to the slaughter. Summer sighed.

"OK, everyone, I won't keep you long," Dominic announced as everyone stood quietly around him in an arc. "I just wanted to say thank you for all your efforts tonight. I know we were in the weeds for a while back there, but you all kept your heads and the guests didn't guess that anything was untoward. We had a calm, professional service, and that's thanks to you all. Well done, have a good rest, and I'll see you again tomorrow night. Thank you."

Everyone clapped and then made their way toward the door. Summer held her breath, expecting him to hold her back.

A few seconds passed. Dominic turned and started chatting with Heaven. Eventually he looked up to see her waiting for him.

"Summer. How was your first service at Collar and Cuffs?" He was actually smiling.

"Er...um...good, I think." She swayed on her feet a bit.

"Great. Heaven and I think you did a splendid job.

I'll see you back here tomorrow night then. Half past six for the briefing, all right?"

Summer was stunned. "Yes, thank you." She turned and left the room before he could change his mind. Her heart raced as she followed the rest of the staff out toward reception and climbed in the elevator.

"I told you he wasn't about to fire you," Heaven whispered, nudging her.

Summer smiled. "I don't know what you told him but whatever it was thank you. He seemed to think I did well tonight."

"You did great," another co-worker, Tuesday, told her in a broad Irish accent. "You certainly gave us all a good laugh. I've never seen Dominic look so stunned as he did when you told him he was scary."

All the staff in the elevator started laughing, and this time Summer laughed with them. "Well he is," she protested.

Summer was one of the last to leave the changing room, having changed back into her smart summer dress and flat shoes. She literally moaned as her bare feet slipped into her cool peep-toes.

"You'll get used to the aching feet," a pretty young girl with a black bun told her with a smile.

"I've never worn heels to wait on before," Summer told her.

"I know. It's crazy isn't it? House rules, I'm afraid. Apart from in the Bottom Bar where you have to go barefoot. Much easier, believe me. I'm April, by the way. You're Summer, right?"

She nodded. "The Bottom Bar! *Damn*, I forgot! Nice to meet you, April. I'll see you tomorrow night. I've gotta go. I just remembered I've got a date tonight." Summer grabbed her purse and headed for the door.

"Bye."

She could hear April giggling as she ran for the elevator. As soon as the door opened Summer shot inside, barging past someone on the way in, and stood panting against the back wall.

"In a hurry?"

Summer recognized the voice before she dared look at his face. Dominic Ray!

"Sorry. Yes. I forgot I've got a date tonight. He'll be waiting," she spluttered nervously.

She heard a chuckle from deep within his throat. "You're not married either, then?"

Summer blushed.

"Do you have a theory on why not?" he went on.

Her mouth went dry. "Well, I...um—"

"Ground floor?"

She realized that they hadn't even moved yet.

"Um, I'm not sure. I'm meeting him at the Bottom Bar. Is that the ground floor?"

Summer watched her boss's demeanor change in an instant. He tensed right up and stared down at her. "Meeting whom?" he demanded.

"Um... a guy I met earlier. Brad, Brad Dexter. Do you

know him?" She felt herself go hot but didn't quite know why. He sure was mad about something.

"Yes, I know him. Did he tell you to meet him there?" Dominic had a face like thunder.

"Yes. He said to come find him there when I was free. I am free now, right?"

"You are free to leave the building. You are *not* free to visit the Bottom Bar." He spoke through gritted teeth as he keyed in the ground floor.

"Oh. I didn't know." Her voice was small, and she felt like she wanted to cry. Not because she really wanted to go for a drink but because she had annoyed Dominic Ray. Her face was hot, and she purposely looked away from him as she felt tears prick the inside of her eyes.

They were only traveling from one floor to the next, but it felt like she was in that elevator for hours. She breathed deeply and blinked, trying to think of anything except the guy standing next to her. She could smell his faint, spicy aftershave and feel his wrath. She noticed his fists clench and wondered why he was so mad at her. Finally there was a pinging sound, and the doors opened. He stood back, allowing her to get out.

"Good night," she muttered as she passed him.

"Good night, Summer. Have a safe journey home."

She turned back just as the doors were closing and noticed he hadn't followed her. She blinked back angry, embarrassed tears as she strode through the reception area and welcomed the bite of cold air as she left Collar and Cuffs.

Chapter Two

The following night Summer entered her workplace feeling a lot more confident. She had given herself a darn good talking-to and was determined not to let anyone upset her or embarrass her tonight. She was also going to try to keep her mouth shut so Dominic Ray would have no reason to speak to her. She would work really hard and try to get as many tips as she could. Lord knows she needed the money.

"Good evening, staff. It's nice to see you all looking bright and happy tonight. We're expecting another busy service, though hopefully not quite as hectic as last night.

"The soup of the day is minestrone, so don't forget to prepare enough Parmesan for your station, and vegetables for the table d'hôte menu are broiled asparagus tips, broccoli florets, and julienned carrots. I'm afraid the lavender streusel with orange crème from the à la carte menu is eighty-six tonight. If Chef manages to come up with a replacement dish I will let you know in due course. Be warned that we may have one or two VIPs in later. If they're going to be on your station I'll let you know, and you'll need to get their meals done on the fly.

"Lastly, Summer is here for her second night tonight, so I'd like April to work with her."

April gave a little yelp of excitement and Summer smiled.

"OK everybody, to your usual stations please, and let's have a good service." Dominic finished off, and they all went straight to their places.

"I'm glad I'm with you tonight. This is going to be fun," April said gleefully.

She was a very pretty, petite girl with what appeared to be shoulder-length hair tied in a tight bun.

"If there's anything you need to know just shout. Shall I show you where to get the Parmesan first?"

Summer was relieved April was so pleased to be working with her. She actually felt like she was going to make some good friends here.

They prepared some small bowls of the cheese and stored them ready. Next April showed her where to find all the various sauces that might be required to accompany different dishes and then where to get the fresh bread.

When they returned to their station Dominic was waiting for them. He didn't look happy.

"Your dumbwaiter is untidy, and we've already got the first four covers in," he told them firmly. "This is not good enough. Summer, you have spilled Parmesan on your skirt. Get in the kitchen and clean it immediately. April, your serving cloths should be neatly folded at all times. Do it now. Then you need to set table twenty-two up for six covers. Your guests are due in five minutes." He stalked away leaving the girls blushing.

"Get cleaned up quick. I'll sort this out," April said hurriedly. She rolled her dark brown eyes heavenward, smiling conspiratorially at her new friend.

Summer rushed into the kitchen, bumping into one of the sous-chefs just by the door.

"I'm so sorry," she gasped, feeling flustered and embarrassed.

"Slow down," the guy told her calmly.

She went over to the tap and quickly ran a cloth under it, which she then used to rub her skirt. The cheese smeared across the fabric.

"Oh no!" she cried, feeling her face go even hotter as she began to tremble.

"Calm down." Heaven was beside her in an instant.

"But I've got customers in five minutes and look at this mess." All her resolve to do well and not get embarrassed tonight had already flown out of the window, and they hadn't even started service yet!

"Here." Heaven took a knife and gently scraped the gooey mess from her skirt and then dabbed it down.

"Thank you so much." Summer felt near to tears.

"Less haste more speed. Don't let it get to you. Just calm down and you'll be fine." Heaven gave her a friendly hug, and Summer took a deep breath before going back to the restaurant.

She noticed April had already seated their guests at table twenty-two, which was now laid for six covers, and she was joking with them as she explained the menu. Feeling totally inadequate, Summer looked over to see Dominic scowling at her from his position across the room. This was going to be a long night.

The service was busy again, as promised, and Summer felt quite tired by the time they had seated the last of their guests. She forced herself to smile as she chatted with them and served their meals.

"You've got two covers coming in five minutes," Dominic murmured in her ear just as she was serving coffee to her last guests.

She must have looked as annoyed as she felt, because he appeared a little taken aback by her expression. She sighed without thinking. She wanted to say, "Fancy coming this late... Can't you tell them we're closed?"

"And lose the attitude," he whispered through gritted teeth.

Summer felt herself glow red hot again, and she clenched her jaw tightly before she could answer him back. She still hadn't forgiven him for tearing into them for an untidy station earlier when it was he who had allowed guests in five minutes before service was supposed to start.

He had then told her off for having spilled Parmesan,

when, in her opinion, the kitchen staff should be preparing cheese.

He had told her *twice* tonight to hurry up when she was waiting for food to be passed over in the kitchen as if it was her fault.

Now he was allowing customers in after closing time!

Her mood only got worse when she saw her guests arrive. Brad Dexter looked dashing in a smart tuxedo, and his date wore a gorgeous low-cut red dress that showed off her slim figure beautifully.

Summer felt a thud in her gut. She hadn't managed to apologize to Brad yet for not joining him in the Bottom Bar last night, and now here he was already with someone else. Not that she had actually considered their arrangement last night to be a real date as such, but she felt this was rubbing her nose in it a little.

"I'm sorry about..." she began as she handed him the menu.

"What's the soup?" He cut her off as though she hadn't spoken.

"Um... minestrone. Look, about... "

"And the vegetables?" He still hadn't taken his eyes off the menu, let alone acknowledged her.

Summer felt anger burn in the pit of her stomach, and she gritted her teeth. April must have noticed her tense up as she stepped in quickly and went through the menu with them.

"Thank you, April." Brad looked up when she had

finished and nodded to indicate that he had finished with her services.

"What a prick!" Summer whispered when April joined her at the dumbwaiter.

"Shh." April put a finger to her lips. "Do you know who he is?"

"Unfortunately, yes. He's Brad Dexter." Summer sneered.

"That's right. Son of Roland Dexter, the guy who owns this place," April explained as they polished more cutlery.

Summer gaped. She looked back over at Brad who was sharing a joke with his date. The boss's son asked her out? As she was gawping at him, Brad turned to face her. He was a very handsome guy, and she could see why he would be pissed at her for not turning up last night. *Shit.* She could also see that he was in no mood to listen to her explanation or apology though, so she nudged her friend.

"Will you take their order? I don't think he likes me."

April chuckled, pulling her order book from her pocket. "Of course. What happened—did you say something about why he's not married?" The black-haired girl giggled and went to take the order.

Summer finished with the cutlery and tidied up an already tidy cupboard just to keep herself busy.

"Two filet mignon coming up," she heard April say cheerfully as she took the menus from the guests.

"Did you say filet mignon?" Summer whispered as

her friend placed the menus on the shelf of the dumb-waiter. "They're eighty-six."

April frowned. "Are you sure?"

"Yes. They told me in the kitchen earlier." "*Damn!*" April sighed and took the menus out again. "This is going to go down like a lead balloon."

She went back to the table where Brad was deep in conversation, although Summer got the impression he was just making April wait in order to be awkward.

"I'm really sorry. I've just been told that the filet is off the menu. Would you like to choose an alternative?" She handed back the menus.

"No, I would not!" Brad's raised voice caused everyone to turn and stare at him. "If a dish is off the menu shouldn't that have been explained *before* the guests made their choice?"

Summer felt herself go hot as she realized that this was her fault. She walked over to the table. "That was my fault, I'm afraid. I forgot to mention it."

Brad gave her a disgusted look and sneered. "You *forgot*? You seem to have a very short memory, don't you?"

"What seems to be the problem here?" Dominic's calm but firm voice broke in, and Summer felt herself go even hotter.

"You seem to be hiring some very incompetent staff these days, Ray," Brad told him disparagingly.

· · ·

Summer felt her knuckles tense, and she was ready to deck the smarmy bastard right then and there.

Dominic looked questioningly at Summer, who was seething.

"It was just a mistake. Summer forgot to mention that the filet mignon was eighty-six before the guests ordered. I didn't realize and took the order," April explained in a sweet voice.

Dominic stared at Summer. "Who told you the filet was eighty-six?"

Summer felt a thud in her stomach. Something wasn't right here. "Th- the exp… Oh no!" She put her hands to her mouth as she suddenly remembered that this was a message she had been given *last* night, not tonight.

Dominic was still gaping at her questioningly. "I'm so sorry. I got muddled up with last night. The filet was off yesterday, not today. I made a mistake." Summer felt physically sick now.

Dominic swiftly took the menus from the guests.

"So there isn't a problem. April, get the order to the kitchen right away. Tell them we want it on the fly."

"Yes, Sir." April threw Summer a sympathetic look and scurried off.

"Sorry about that," Dominic told Brad and the woman, with a smile that Summer guessed wasn't real.

She opened her mouth to apologize again, but Dominic threw her a look that made her reconsider. He handed her the menus and stalked off.

Summer placed the menus neatly on the shelf and, keeping her back to the table, busied herself with tidying up the cutlery again. She could feel the eyes of everyone in the room boring into her, and she made a conscious effort not to look at anyone.

Her heart was pounding, and she felt hot and flushed. She fought back embarrassed tears as she forced herself to keep busy.

"Don't you have a wine list to offer us?" Brad's sarcasm ripped into her thoughts, and she turned around quickly. She had completely forgotten to offer them drinks. He and his date sat staring derisively at her.

"Of course." She carefully took the lists and offered them over.

"What would you recommend?" Brad asked without even opening the drinks menu. "It's to accompany filet mignon. Or at least we hope it is!"

The woman in the red dress giggled, and Brad sneered.

Summer took a deep breath as her ire inched up yet another notch. "Châteauneuf-du-Pape would be perfect," she informed him without studying the wine list.

Brad raised his eyebrows in obvious surprise. "Good choice," he murmured. "All right, we'll have a bottle."

"Thank you." Summer gave them her sickliest smile and retrieved the menus just as April arrived with their appetizers.

"Everything OK?" The dark-haired girl asked as she joined Summer back at the dumbwaiter.

"Yeah. I just have to get the wine," Summer said with a sigh.

"Right." April smiled as Summer rolled her eyes and went to the bar.

"Châteauneuf-du-Pape?" The bartender looked impressed. "Well done. Even Darren, the sommelier, doesn't sell much of that—when he can be bothered to turn up for work, that is."

Summer was trembling so much that she was afraid she would spill the wine all over Brad, so she busied herself with the food while the barman served their drinks.

Fortunately they didn't stay around for desserts, and as Dominic had dismissed the rest of the staff once they had all finished serving, Summer and April were allowed to go without even laying the table afterward.

"I'm so sorry about tonight," Summer said as April quickly changed.

"Don't worry about it. Nobody died." Her friend grinned.

"Brad fucking Dexter nearly did!" Summer told her. "I was ready to kill him with my own bare hands. I mean, it's one thing to make a mistake, but does he have to be so damn rude?"

"Don't let it worry you." April laughed "I'll see you tomorrow."

"If I've still got a job by then." Summer waved gloomily as her friend disappeared out the door.

Alone in the quiet changing room, Summer took a deep breath as she changed into her jeans. With just her thoughts for company she felt herself sink into a state of depression, and she found tears streaming down her hot face. What a night.

She was beginning to think that Colin Cromer, her ex, was completely right about her being useless. She couldn't get anything right.

She sniffed and found a tissue in her purse, which she put to good use, before deciding that she had made one big mistake in coming here. She had hoped that getting a decent job in a nice part of the city would be a new start for her, and a great disguise. No one would think of looking for her here.

But now she realized this was because she really didn't belong here. She was way out of her depth.

She quickly popped into the bathroom and washed her face before grabbing her purse and heading back toward the elevator.

As it was well past midnight and most of the staff had gone home, Summer was surprised to hear shouting coming from one of the offices on her way.

"Well, it looks like you need to start looking for a new maître d' then." Dominic's steady voice stopped Summer in her tracks.

She followed the sound of voices, stopping in the corridor a few doors from where they were coming from.

"Bullshit!" Dominic was clearly angry, but his raised voice was still precise and coherent.

Summer felt her stomach lurch as she feared he was losing his job because of her incompetence. Tears started streaming down her face again, and she felt sick.

"Should you be listening to this?" A deep voice came from behind her, and she shot around to see the blurry face of a rather tall man who had collar-length dark wavy hair and stubble on his chin. He wore a smart gray suit. She blinked as she gazed into his handsome face and noticed his large, warm brown eyes. It was that guy again —the one from the foyer and the restaurant.

"We just seem to keep running into one another," she sobbed.

"Hey. Are you all right?" He put a comforting arm around her.

She shook her head and snuggled into his embrace as he led her into a nearby office.

"It's all my fault," she whispered as he handed her a tissue from a box on the desk.

"I doubt that very much." He chuckled. "Now why don't you dry your eyes and tell me what this is all about?"

They sat side by side on a small sofa at the back of the room while she composed herself. His large, warm hand covered one of hers while she wiped her face with the other.

"I think Dominic is losing his job because of me. He hired me yesterday, and I embarrassed him in the restaurant by telling him that I thought he wasn't married because he was so scary—which he is—well, you saw what happened, and then tonight I got it all wrong in front of the boss's son. I think he's in there getting fired right now."

She wiped her face and looked up into two twinkling eyes.

"This is Dominic Ray, right? Master D? The maître d' from the restaurant?"

His lips were slightly turned up at the edges, but Summer couldn't see anything to smile about.

She nodded. "Yes. He's my boss. Or he was. I thought he was going to fire me last night and then again tonight. Only it looks like *he's* the one being fired. It's all my fault."

"Is that why you were listening to their conversation in the corridor?" His face was kind, but also firm, and she felt herself flush with embarrassment.

She shook her head. "I was on my way to find him to resign. I'm not cut out for working here. Only, I heard him shouting and when I got here..."

"I see." His voice was low and deep and oozed confidence. He looked thoughtful for a moment. "I think we should talk to Master D, er, I mean Dominic about this."

Summer stared up at him, wide-eyed. "He'll hate me. I've done nothing but cause trouble since I got here."

He snickered. "I'm sure that's not true."

She wished she shared his conviction but said nothing.

"Come on," he said, standing up and pulling her with him. "Let's get this sorted."

Summer gazed up at the gorgeous hunk. He was a little more rugged than Dominic, and she felt a little easier in his company. He was quite a commanding character, but he had an air of fairness about him that she admired.

Her hand was still in his as he led her out of the room, and they stopped in front of the managing director's office just as the door opened.

"Hey Nathan. What are you doing here? And what in hell is *she* doing here?" Brad's face contorted as he caught sight of Summer, and she felt herself shrink back nervously.

"Resigning, I think," the guy, who was evidently called Nathan, replied matter-of-factly.

"Is that right?" She heard Dominic's voice in the background and wished she'd just gone home after all. He didn't sound happy.

The door opened wider, and Brad took a step back to allow them to enter the room.

"Good evening, gentlemen. I'm sorry to intrude. I found this upset young lady in the corridor, and I thought she should come speak with you."

Nathan shook hands with Dominic and Brad as the other guy, an older man with gray hair and glasses, stood up from behind the large desk. He leaned over and shook hands with Nathan before indicating to them all to sit down.

"Mr. Dexter, this is Summer Marsden," Dominic introduced her, and she saw a knowing look cross the older man's face as she shook his large, warm hand.

"So you're Summer. It's nice to meet you," he said with a grin.

Summer flushed and took a seat in between Nathan and Dominic.

"I think you should join us for this, Brad," his father told him as he paced the floor near the doorway, evidently deciding whether to stay after all.

Brad looked like a petulant child as his father stared at him, waiting expectantly. Finally he took a seat the other side of Dominic.

"Well, young lady. Welcome to Collar and Cuffs," the older man said, tearing his eyes from his son and settling them on her.

She swallowed hard.

"I hear you've been settling in quite well. Even got my son to part with his cash for a bottle of our best Châteauneuf-du-Pape this evening." He chuckled.

Summer shifted a little uneasily in her chair but didn't speak.

"Yeah, after botching up my steak order!" Brad sneered.

"She did not botch anything up. She made an honest mistake because she was tired and nervous, that's all," Dominic corrected him through gritted teeth.

Summer stared at her boss in astonishment, but

Dominic's straight, calm face was pointed toward the MD.

"Well, I'm not surprised she was nervous. It was only her second night, after all," Mr. Dexter said kindly.

Summer smiled gratefully.

"It was nothing to do with that," Dominic interjected. "She was nervous because your son made her feel nervous." He was still staring straight ahead.

"Oh yeah, and how did I manage that? I hardly spoke to her," Brad jeered.

"Exactly my point," Dominic replied coolly. "You broke club rules last night by asking a newcomer to join you for a drink in the Bottom Bar, and when she wasn't allowed to attend, you refused to allow her to explain or apologize. You did all you could to make her feel uncomfortable tonight. That is *not* how we treat submissives in this club, and you know it. You were completely out of order." This time Dominic turned to face Brad, whose face went bright red.

Summer felt a jolt in her stomach. *Submissives?* How did they know? She opened her mouth to object, but Nathan placed a calming hand over hers and she turned to face him. He was smiling slightly, and the twinkle was back in his eyes.

She felt indignant and annoyed but closed her mouth without speaking. She was well aware that her big mouth usually landed her in trouble.

"Quite right, Dominic. Bradley, what have you got to

say for yourself?" Mr. Dexter's kind eyes had turned quite pale and cool as he challenged his son.

"How was I to know she was a newcomer? I didn't know she wasn't a member." He sulked, slumping farther into his chair.

"All the more reason why you shouldn't have invited her to the Bottom Bar," his father replied.

Brad sighed irritably.

"Dominic, did you explain to Summer why she wasn't allowed to join Bradley in the bar?" The older man's eyes turned to her boss, and she felt herself flush.

"No. It was very remiss of me, I know, but I didn't explain. I just forbade her from going to meet him." Dominic wasted no time in admitting his guilt. "I apologize, Summer. It was unfair and wrong of me to treat you like that." His eyes found hers, and he spoke with genuine sincerity.

"No wonder I thought she'd stood me up." Brad moaned.

"Shut up, Bradley," his father snapped. He turned back to Summer who was finding it hard to look at Dominic and had resorted to fiddling with the denim of her jeans.

"Miss Marsden. I can see that you have been treated very unfairly during your short time with us here at Collar and Cuffs. I would like to add my apologies as, I am sure, would my son." He gave Bradley a meaningful look, and his son huffed.

"I'm sorry. I shouldn't have assumed that you had

stood me up, and I should have been more respectful to you tonight." Brad looked straight at Summer as he apologized, and she blushed again.

"Thank you," she whispered.

"And you can steer clear of the club restaurant for a while too, Bradley. I think you've caused enough trouble there." The old man frowned at his son before managing a smile for the rest of them.

"Right, well, now we've got that sorted I suggest we all adjourn to the bar. Miss Marsden, would you like to join us in the Bottom Bar for a nightcap as my guest? We can lend you some clothes?"

Summer felt her heart lift, and a burn seared the pit of her stomach. "Yes please, Sir."

He smiled. "Master Nathan, as it was you who brought her to us, perhaps you would like to accompany Miss Marsden to the bar and help her out? We'll join you down there shortly."

Nathan smiled and nodded at the boss before helping Summer out of her chair. He stood back and followed her to the door, and she felt his strong hand on the small of her back, guiding her toward the elevator.

"Have you been to a BDSM club before?" he asked when they were in the elevator.

Summer felt a rush of excitement. "Yes, Sir." She didn't know why she automatically called him "Sir" but it just felt right somehow. Probably old habits, she told herself.

"Locally?"

She suddenly felt her face drain as she realized he was expecting her to talk about herself and her past.

"No, not in Miami," she confessed.

His questioning look told her he wasn't content with her answer.

"I went to a couple near Daytona Beach a few years back," she told him.

He nodded. "Did you enjoy it there?"

"Very much." She smiled as memories of happier times came flooding back to her mind. "So why stop going?"

"I had to move with work," she told him simply. "I got a great job opportunity in Fort Lauderdale. I worked in a really nice restaurant there for a while. The shifts were real long though, and I didn't get time to go visit any clubs."

Nathan nodded, smiling. "Whereas here you get the best of both worlds." The doors opened and Summer gasped.

The lower floor was nothing like the rest of the building. Music thumped down the corridor from somewhere, and she could already hear people laughing and shouting. The club evidently took up the whole floor.

A large sign faced the elevator with the words "Collar and Cuffs." This time, however, the picture was of a woman in the submissive pose with a collar of ownership around her neck and her hands fastened behind her back with handcuffs.

She felt Nathan's hand in the center of her back again as he led her down a corridor.

A short, plump girl was walking toward them wearing a little pink skirt, which didn't quite cover her bare behind, and a black bra top. She had bare feet and long, blonde hair. She was very pretty, and she smiled as she neared them.

"Good evening, Hope. This is Summer. She's new here."

Hope beamed at her, and Summer instantly liked her.

"Could you find something for her to wear for me, then show her through to the bar?"

"Of course, Master Nathan." She nodded and then took Summer by the arm.

"I'll see you soon." Nathan winked as Summer smiled nervously at him and then followed Hope down another corridor.

"Don't look so worried, no one's going to hurt you. Unless you ask real nicely," Hope nudged her with a giggle.

Summer laughed. "I've just been asked to come down for a drink, really. I don't know why I have to change."

"House rules." Hope smiled. "I guess people might feel a little awkward if they were undressed while others walked around in normal clothes."

"I see your point," Summer agreed as they entered a large changing room. Ladies stood around talking, in various stages of undress, while others were changing in front of their lockers or the large mirrors that lined two of the massive walls.

"You can use this locker," Hope told her as she pointed to a large metal one, and she went to fetch her something to wear while Summer began to undress.

"Are you sure about this?" Summer frowned as Hope returned with a short blue skirt and a white crop top.

"Of course. You don't want to look out of place, do you?" Hope grinned.

Summer quickly changed, hoping that her skirt was long enough to cover her backside. It was—just. Promising herself that she would sit on a bar stool all night so no one would see her bare butt, she followed Hope out into the bar.

"How long have you worked here?" Summer asked as they walked through.

She tried not to stare at the submissives, some of whom were completely naked. She also remembered to lower her eyes when she came near a Dom or Domme.

"Only a few months down here, but I work upstairs in the restaurant too. I've been up there for a couple of years now," Hope explained.

Summer's eyes widened. "So it's OK to do both?"

"Yeah, of course. Only submissives can work down here though, hence the name, of course, the Bottom Bar." She smiled. "Master Nathan is at the bar right over there. Have a nice night."

Summer nodded and looked over to where Hope indicated. She had thought Nathan was a good-looking guy earlier but here, in a black satin shirt partially open—revealing his chest hair—and tight black leather trousers, he looked stunning. He had a real hungry look in his eyes, a look she'd seen many times before. A drink seemed to be the last thing on his mind. She gasped.

Chapter Three

Nathan's face lit up when he saw the pretty little sub walking slowly toward him. She looked really sweet in a short skirt and little top, which showed a lot more of her soft flesh than that T-shirt and jeans she was wearing earlier. He couldn't help noticing she seemed a little self-conscious. Too sexy.

"You look nice," he told her, standing up as she arrived at the bar.

"Thank you, Sir."

He noticed she wasn't looking at his face. Her eyes were down, and she had a serene air about her.

She obviously knew the correct way to act in a club. He was impressed.

"You can look at me, Summer." He used a finger to tilt her head up so she stared straight into his eyes. Her bright green eyes shone, and her face had an excited yet controlled expression. Quite charming.

"Thank you, Sir ." Her mouth was moist, and her lips looked beautifully soft and lush. He just wanted to kiss them then and there.

Clearing his throat, he gestured to her to climb onto the stool next to him, and he watched carefully as the little skirt rode up her thighs even farther, confirming that she wasn't wearing underwear. He felt a satisfied smile cross his lips. Good girl!

"What can I get you?" he asked, sitting down next to her.

"Coke, please ."

The bartender nodded.

He looked back to her and noticed that she had one hand on the bar while the other covered her soft stomach. He grinned to himself. Shame she wasn't confident about that gorgeous round body of hers. He considered making her move that arm but then thought better of it. After all, they had only just met and this was her first time in a club for a while.

He took the glass from the bartender and passed it over to her.

"Thank you." It wasn't much more than a whisper.

He took a swig of his beer while she stared around the large room. Someone screamed her orgasm from the St. Andrew's Cross, and Summer glanced over.

In another corner the glow of a violet wand shone through the dim light, while at another station the spanking horse was being put to good use.

Watching her expression, he was agreeably surprised

that she didn't seem shocked or horrified by what she was looking at. She took it all in her stride.

"Tell me about your past experience." He purposely kept his voice low, hoping to ease more information from her that way.

She looked back to him, and he could then see she hadn't been unaffected by the sights and sounds around her. Her face was slightly flushed, and her eyes sparkled with excitement.

"I haven't been for a couple of years," she explained, sipping her Coke.

"Did you have a Dom?"

"Not a regular one. I used to play with different ones."

"I see. And after you left did you miss it?"

Her eyes went even wider. "Yes, Sir. I wanted to go to another one but..."

He detected a sadness in her face and guessed that work wasn't the only thing keeping her from the clubs. After waiting patiently for her to continue for a few minutes, he realized she wasn't willing to divulge her reasons.

"Did you have a boyfriend in Fort Lauderdale?" He knew the answer by the look on her face.

"Yes, Sir."

"Was he into the lifestyle?"

She shook her head with a grimace. "No."

"What did he do?"

Suddenly her face clouded over, and she looked away

quickly. It made his heart ache to see her expression like that.

"For a living? A job?" he clarified.

She slowly raised her head again, and he saw that her face was red and hot. Her eyes were close to tears, and she bit her lip a little nervously.

"Oh, I see. He worked on a construction site for a while. Manual labor." She sniffed and quickly looked away as if embarrassed.

Nathan put his hand on hers. She was trembling and felt hot. He knew there was a lot she wasn't telling him, and suddenly he wanted to know everything.

If someone had hurt this beautiful creature he wanted to know who, so he could go and rip his fucking head off.

It would have to wait though. Roland Dexter would be here soon, and Nathan didn't want the boss to find her upset again. Especially as it would be *his* fault this time.

"So what do you like doing? Cross or bench? Paddle or whip? Any intense stuff?" He tried to sound light and friendly to change the mood a little. He was also desperate to find out what this gorgeous little sub was into so they could have some fun. His cock twitched at the thought. He had already seen that she was an expressive little thing and guessed she would be very responsive to his ministrations.

She shrugged, looking around again. "Either. No needles though. I hate those."

"Want to take a look around?" he offered, noticing the boss entering the room with Brad and Dominic.

They had all changed and were looking around at what few subs were left. It was quite late and most had gone home already.

"Sure." Her eyes lit up, and he helped her down from the stool. He was rewarded with a flash of her soft thigh, which made his cock jerk again, and he was suddenly aware of how swollen he was.

Nathan deliberately led her away from the doorway, hoping to avoid the boss for a while. He was grateful Dexter had given him the opportunity to bring her down here, but he felt very possessive of the fragile little sub and wanted to keep her for himself.

"Hi, Nathan." Dan, one of the Doms, stopped them as they neared the St. Andrew's Cross.

"Master Dan, I'd like you meet Summer."

She automatically dipped her head politely.

"Hey Summer, I haven't seen you here before."Dan smiled.

She didn't speak, and Nathan realized she must be used to a quite high protocol.

"She's new." He noticed a look of admiration from Dan and suddenly felt the urge to punch his lights out. *And mine, for the time being, at least.*

"We need to discuss rosters for this place when you get a minute," Dan told him. "A couple of the subs have got vacations coming up, so we might be a bit short staffed."

"OK," Nathan said with a sigh.

Dan looked toward the door. "The boss is here. I need to catch him for a quick word. See you later. Nice meeting you, Summer."

She smiled, and Nathan was sure he saw her flush slightly. Dan was a good-looking Dom and very popular with the subs. He was also a good friend to Nathan. And he could stay a good friend, by keeping his hands off his girl.

As if reading his mind, Dan smirked as he walked away. Nathan snorted and put a possessive arm around Summer, pulling her close to him. Her soft, round body melted into his side, and he was sure he heard her sigh. He smiled as a warm feeling flooded his insides.

After showing her around the large room, Nathan decided he still wasn't ready to share her, so he guided her down a corridor that led off the main area.

She had taken an interest in everything so far, and he was feeling the strain as his cock ached and throbbed in the tight confines of his leathers. He had also noticed a lot of admiring glances as he'd led her around and was surprised at how annoyed he was that the other Doms and Dommes were eyeing up his sub.

His sub? Christ, they'd only just met. Still, she seemed to just fit so well with him, and he'd loved everything about her since the moment he first saw her.

Her smile, her voice, her laugh, and even her fresh, clean smell. Her short, spiky hair was softer than it looked and smelled of honey. It framed her beautiful, round face perfectly and gave her a cute, endearing look. Her eyes were big and expressive. She wasn't going to be able to hide anything from him. Even her body flushed and tensed at the sight of some of the scenes, indicating how much she was aroused by the events around her.

Nathan was pleased he could read her so well. After releasing his last sub, Sharon, he wondered if he wasn't losing his touch. He thought he could read any sub until he realized how much she was holding out on him. She had managed to string him along for over a year, letting him believe that she was happy with him and that all she ever wanted to do was to serve him. He had done all he could to look after her, care for her, and give her everything she said she wanted. Heck, he even loved her! He thought she felt the same. She *said* she did. Then one day she just up and left.

He had been stunned. She had never discussed it with him, she just packed her things and left him a note telling him that it wasn't working out for her and that she had found someone who was willing to give her what she needed. He wondered how he could have been so stupid.

That question haunted him for months afterward. Then he had just come to the club and found a different sub to play with each night. No sex was involved. He never promised them anything and never expected anything from them. It was just a mutual understanding, the fulfillment of a need for a few hours. The subs seemed happy with it. He was happy with it. Until now.

He studied the little sub who was now trembling at his side. What the...?

"Sorry, sugar. You don't like needle-play do you?" He suddenly realized that he had wandered down to the specialist playrooms and had paused outside the "surgery." It looked like the Dom was using some kind of acupuncture on his male sub's body, and Summer was silently cringing at the sight.

"How about fire-play?"

She looked up at him, her eyes wide. She nodded slowly.

"Ever done it?"

"No, Sir. I've seen it a few times, though."

"What did you think of it?"

"I thought it looked... interesting."

"Good enough." He chuckled and led her to a room a little farther on.

Blue flames were caressing a sub's slender stomach, and she had a peaceful look on her face. He watched Summer's expression. She sure looked intrigued by it, and he made a mental note to bear it in mind.

"Water sports?" he asked after a few minutes. She pulled a face, shaking her head. "No, thank you."

He laughed. "Good job. Me neither," he confessed, pulling a face back.

She giggled. It was a sweet, tinkling sound.

"OK, how about the schoolroom? Wanna see someone getting caned?"

Summer shrugged. "I don't mind, Sir. Surely it's the same as on the cross or spanking horse, though?"

"You're not really into role-play, are you?" He studied her closely.

She swallowed. "Not really, Sir." She seemed a little embarrassed.

"That's OK. How about we head back to the bar, in that case?"

She smiled and nodded. "OK—I mean, yes, Sir."

He couldn't resist pulling her a little closer to him and relished the way her body molded into his.

As they went back into the bar, Nathan noticed the spanking horse was free and had a sign on it indicating that it had been cleaned ready for use. He felt a flutter in his stomach when he saw that Summer was looking at it too, with a faraway look in her eyes. His cock twitched yet again.

"Fancy a go?" He murmured in her ear and felt her whole body come alive in his arms.

She stared up at him with hopeful eyes. "Could we... I mean... Are we allowed...um...yes, Sir. Yes, please," she stammered.

He snickered. There weren't many people around now as it was so late, and he felt it was the perfect time to introduce her to the delights of the facilities.

"Anything I need to know about? I mean, I know we haven't actually gone through your limits or anything. Any medical conditions?" He watched her face as he asked her and saw a totally serene expression.

"No, Sir. My safe word is 'banana'." He saw total honesty in her face and relief swept through him. She certainly wore her heart on her sleeve, and he was confident that she wouldn't try to pull the wool over his eyes.

"Banana it is, then." He nodded with a smile. "No problems with being bound?" He had helped her up onto the horse and was about to cuff her hands and feet.

She laid her face against the soft leather of the horse as though resting it on a feather pillow. "No problems at all, Sir." She smiled.

Nathan clipped on the cuffs, running his finger around the inside to ensure a comfortable fit. Her skin was so soft and smooth he wanted to touch her all the time. His cock told him it was time to stop though, so he obeyed.

He took a minute to drink in the sight of her lying across the contraption. Her neck looked long and elegant, and her legs were silky and delectable. Her whole body was softness personified, and he loved it.

He ran his hands up and down her legs, lifting the short skirt up to reveal her smooth, round butt. He stroked her back gently and felt her sink into the horse with a contented sigh. He had never known a sub to be so relaxed on their first time with him. He could feel the trust emanating from her, and he cherished it.

Suddenly he smacked her warm, soft butt, and she yelped in surprise. He did it again five times, and watched her close her eyes, as if letting the sting wash over her as he smoothed it away afterward. He swatted her another five times, and instead of tensing up, he felt her relax even more into the leather.

"Good girl," he cooed and watched a smile spread across her lips. She responded well to compliments, he noted.

Another five swats followed by his hand holding in the heat and then gently rubbing away the sting. Then another. And another.

Nathan felt his own tension release as he played, watching her body and her face closely for her reaction. Tears streamed down her beautiful face after a while, but she didn't make a sound, except to confirm she was OK when he asked her.

He varied the position of his hand and felt her wetness when he swatted her up from the base of her butt. He smiled as he saw her body tense at last and watched her breathing become more rasping. His finger swiped her clit.

"Come for me, Summer," he murmured softly into her ear as a look of pure delight crossed her face.

Immediately she opened her eyes and stared at him as she screamed her release. It was the most beautiful sight he had seen in his life, and he felt his cock strain hard against his leathers. His release would have to wait though. He quickly clicked open the cuffs and lifted her quivering body into his arms. She was a soft handful, and he loved the feel of her so close to him.

She closed her eyes as her arms wrapped instinctively around his neck, and he carried her to a nearby sofa surrounded by artificial plants in a warm, quiet corner of the room. He pulled a blanket from the back of the couch and wrapped it around her sated body, whispering to her all the time.

"You did well, sugar. I'm so proud of you."

Her full lips curved slightly into a contented smile, and she drifted off to sleep in his arms. Nathan gazed into the somnolent face of an angel. His angel.

Summer opened her eyes slowly, not sure where she was. Warm, strong arms held her, and she suddenly realized she was still at Collar and Cuffs.

"Hey beautiful." Nathan's deep voice rippled through his chest next to her ear, and she sat upright.

"I'm sorry," she said, feeling a little embarrassed and a whole lot flustered.

"Why?"

His slight frown marred an otherwise gorgeous face as she stared up at him. From this angle she could see his handsome face with the thin stubble on his chin and cheeks giving him a roguish appearance. His slightly longer, collar-length dark waves gave him a casual air, and the warmth and faint scent of spice were an indication—as if any were needed—that this guy was definitely all man.

"I fell asleep," she whispered.

"I noticed." He laughed softly.

She rolled her eyes at her own daft comment and giggled. Looking around she could see that the place was empty and the lights were low. A sudden panic shot through her.

"What time is it? I have to go."

"Slow down, sugar," he said, holding her tight to stop her leaping from his lap. "Why the hurry?"

"I need to get home. I've got an interview tomorrow... today... well, in the morning." She felt herself go hot as her mind raced, but he was holding her tight.

"OK, calm down. It's just after three. Let's get changed and I'll run you home. What time's your appointment?"

"Six fifteen, but it's across town. It'll take me over an hour to get there." She was calculating the times in her head as she spoke. It took her forty-five minutes to walk here, so she could be home just after four. That would give her time for a quick shower and change before she set off for the interview.

"Come on, let's get changed." His voice was calm as he slowly released her and helped her get up.

She felt a little light-headed and instinctively reached out for him as she felt herself swaying on her feet.

"Wow, sugar. When did you last eat?" He caught her and scooped her up in his muscular arms.

Summer was mortified. She knew she was on the heavy side and must have been breaking his back with her bulk.

"I'm fine. Put me down."

"You're not fine. And I believe I asked you a question." He didn't seem to be struggling with her weight as he walked easily through the empty club and over to the changing rooms.

Her head felt like mush. "I had lunch," she said quietly.

"Lunch? You haven't eaten since yesterday lunchtime? Well no wonder you're not right, sugar. How did you come to miss dinner?"

She felt herself go hot with embarrassment. "I was across town to see about this job," she explained. "It took a whole lot longer than I thought, and I had to get here for six thirty so I got the bus, but it was late and..."

"So you did a full shift upstairs and then exerted yourself down here without a meal inside you?" He shook his head in clear disbelief.

Summer said nothing. She felt stupid. She had done what she had to in order to get to work on time.

She didn't know that Brad fucking Dexter was going to make her have to work late and that afterward Nathan whatever-his-name-was was going to take her to see the boss and then bring her down here and... She felt herself blush and buried her face in his chest.

The smooth satin caressed her cheek, and the soft hairs of his chest tickled her chin. His spicy smell surrounded her, and the memories of the wonderful time they'd had together flooded her mind.

"You OK now?"

They were just outside the women's changing room when he gently lowered her to the floor.

"Yes, thank you, Sir." Her own words shocked her, and she stared up at him.

"Good. You've got five minutes. I'll be waiting here for you. If you take any longer than that I'll be in to find you. Got it?" His warm, brown eyes twinkled with mirth, and she couldn't help smiling as she nodded.

The events of the evening whirled around in her head as she quickly changed. This gorgeous hunk had actually spanked her and made her come in the club. The club where she worked. Sort of. And Dominic and Mr. Dexter and Brad were there! Were they there when it happened?

"*Oh shit!*"

"You OK, sugar?"

She suddenly realized that she had said it aloud and that Mr. Nathan hunk-of-the-year was right outside the door.

"Um... yeah, just coming."

"Again? You're insatiable, woman." He chuckled, and she blushed.

"Sorry, I was just thinking out loud," she explained as she arrived by his side.

He was wearing his suit trousers and his shirt, open, no tie. He held his jacket up on his shoulder with one finger, and he was casually leaning against the doorjamb. Summer felt her breath hitch. Had he really been that handsome earlier?

"What were you thinking?" He put his other arm around her shoulder and led her toward the elevator.

She blushed again. "I was wondering about earlier," she began, staring at her feet instead of his gorgeous face.

"Just what were you wondering about it?" His voice was deep and suggestive, and she felt butterflies dance in her stomach.

"Well, when we...when I..."

He followed her into the elevator. Somehow being there with him in this confined space made it even harder to speak. He stood right up close to her, facing her, and lifted her chin with one finger. She breathed him in with a gasp.

"When I spanked your pretty little butt until you came?" His southern voice was husky and rasping as he practically growled the words out.

She stared into his warm eyes and realized the close proximity of his mouth to hers. She felt his breath on her face, and a fire began to burn in her stomach. A fire, she remembered, which had burned brightly down there earlier when they were in the club together.

"Yes," she whispered.

She felt his nearness as he leaned down and gently grazed his warm, moist lips against hers. She felt sparks of electricity fly between them and gently pressed her mouth to his. His tongue lapped at the seam of her lips until she opened them, and then his jacket fell to the floor as both arms wrapped around her, cloaking her in his warmth, his scent, his body.

His kiss was soft and sensual, and she felt as though she was floating through the air on a cloud of hope.

A pinging sound alerted them that they were on the ground floor, and he slowly loosened his grip.

One arm still held her as he elegantly stooped down to retrieve his jacket when the door opened.

She snuggled into his warmth as the cool air met them in the foyer, and he wrapped his jacket around her before leading her outside.

There was only one car in the management parking lot, and he guided her over to it.

"Where do you live, sugar?" He opened the passenger door for her and she climbed in, grateful she didn't have to endure that long walk home.

The thought of her poky apartment entered her head and she swallowed hard, trying to decide whether to tell him a different address so he wouldn't see where she lived. She was exhausted though, it had been a long night. And that kiss...

"Is it far?"

She was suddenly aware that he had already gone around the car and climbed into the driver's seat.

He turned the key and the engine hummed. She looked around at the plush leather. This car must have cost more than a couple of years' wages for her.

"I'll show you," she said with a sigh.

He smiled. "I had fun tonight. I hope you did too?"

He was looking across at her, and she couldn't help thinking he looked slightly concerned.

"Yes. Thank you. I just wondered whether..." He watched her expectantly.

"Well, were Mr. Dexter and the others there when...?"

Nathan laughed, and his large hand came over and covered hers as she fiddled with the fabric of her jeans.

"I have no idea," he said, shaking his head. "To be honest, they were the last things on my mind."

She stared down into her lap.

"Does it matter?" He must have noticed her uncertainty with the situation as his voice sounded a little anxious.

"Well, Dominic's my boss. I have to work with him, you know?"

"Did you see them there tonight, in the club?" He asked slowly.

"No. I know Master Dan said they'd arrived so they must have showed up, but I don't know how long they stayed. Maybe they left early." She shrugged, immediately feeling happier.

"Maybe." Nathan's warm hand squeezed hers, and she felt a glow of excitement flood her system.

She directed him to her run-down street and pointed out her apartment block. He didn't seem perturbed at all, and she was relieved.

He was obviously quite wealthy and she was embarrassed about where she now lived, but she wasn't going to lie to him about it. What would be the point? He was one of the management team, and she was a waitress. He was also a Dom, and she knew that meant he wasn't going to ridicule her.

He had been really nice to her tonight and that kiss was out of this world, but she wasn't naive enough to think it meant anything. Not to him, anyway.

"I'll walk you up," he said casually as he got out of the car.

It must have been nearly four in the morning, and in this neighborhood she would have been a fool to refuse. Not that she had encountered any trouble herself, but she wasn't about to take any chances.

"It's this one," she told him as they reached her front door. "Do you want some coffee?"

She expected him to say no. Who would blame him? Instead he looked thoughtful.

"Are you having one or were you planning to get some sleep?"

She giggled. "I haven't got time to sleep," she told him. "I'll definitely be having coffee, and lots of it."

He looked surprised. "Well, in that case, I'd love to join you."

The apartment was old and paint peeled from the walls, but it was clean—she made sure of that.

The furniture was bought from a second-hand store, but she had given it all a good wash and it looked all right. At least she thought so. She had made her own curtains with cushions to match, and the kitchen shone.

"This is nice," he said, looking around.

"Thanks. Sit down." She went through and put the

kettle on. The kitchen area was only sectioned off by a counter and some cupboards, so they were easily able to carry on a conversation while she prepared the drinks.

"How long have you lived here?" he asked, looking around.

"A couple of weeks," she told him.

"You've got it really nice."

She felt herself blush. Something about getting his approval seemed to have an unholy effect on her, though she didn't know why.

She handed him his coffee and sat in the chair opposite him. The two chairs and tiny sofa didn't actually match, but she had covered them in matching throws to try to coordinate the look. And to hide the coffee stains, which no amount of fabric cleaner would remove.

She didn't like being so far away from him, she realized, having woken in his embrace and kissed in the elevator.

She told herself it hadn't really meant anything and she was probably just feeling a little emotional because of the circumstances and the long night.

"Did you come here for a job?" he asked.

"No. I only just managed to get the job at the club at the last minute. I thought I'd missed the deadline but Dominic, um, *Master* Dominic, was kind enough to give me an interview.

'I didn't think I'd get it, to be honest. It's been a while since I did silver service." She sipped her coffee.

"So what's the job you're going for today?"

She flushed, wondering if he thought she was about to leave the club. "It's just shelf-stacking in a small grocery store," she explained, stifling a yawn.

His eyes narrowed. "And you'd prefer that to working at the club?"

She stared at him. "Oh no. I love working at the club. It's just that they can only give me a few shifts a week. This job's not great pay but they've said they can offer me full-time work if I want it. Which I don't. I just need to supplement my shifts, that's all."

Nathan nodded. "I see. So how many hours are you going to do in the grocery store?"

Surprised at his interest, Summer put her mug on the coffee table, pulled a notebook from a magazine rack next to her chair, and opened it.

"Well, I've worked out that I've got three regular shifts at the club each week, although Dom...Master Dominic can't tell me which nights I have to do yet. Anyway, Ms. Powell at the grocery store needs me to do at least four shifts there, with the possibility of more as and when I'm needed. They've got staff vacations coming up, and sometimes it gets real busy at weekends too, so I might have to work longer. Anyway, if I do a minimum of three nights at the club and four days in the store, that should cover my rent, bills, and bus fares." She smiled, preening a little.

Nathan came over to where she was sitting and put his mug on the table next to hers. "How many hours are you going to be working, then?"

"Well, I have to be at the club for six hours each night, and the store shifts are eight in the morning until six at night, unless I have to work over. In actual fact I have to get to the store for half past seven because of the bus service, but I don't need to start until eight so I thought I could take my breakfast with me and have it more leisurely once I get over there.

"The only problem might be if Master Dominic and Ms. Powell need me on the same day. Master Dominic wants us to be there for six thirty, but I don't finish at the grocery store until six o'clock and it's too far even by cab to get from one to the other in half an hour. Not that I could afford a cab anyhow."

She bit her lip. When she looked up at Nathan she was surprised at how hard he was frowning.

"But you'd be working a minimum of fifty-eight hours a week, and that's not including traveling time." Nathan shook his head as he looked at her figures. "Even if it was logistically possible, which I doubt, you'd be exhausted."

Summer laughed. "I'm not afraid of hard work, you know. When I was in West Palm Beach I was working over a hundred and..." She coughed uncomfortably. Grabbing the notebook from him she quickly stuffed it back into the rack.

"When was this?" He was studying her closely, and she felt unnerved by him.

"It doesn't matter. Look, I'm sorry. I have to get ready for my interview soon, so..."

"Don't do it," he beseeched her, grabbing her arm as she went to stand up.

"That's OK for you to say, mister megabucks." She snorted. "I'll bet you've never had to work more than one job at a time, have you?"

She was surprised to see the hurt expression on his face and immediately regretted her attitude.

"All I'm saying is…" He sighed as she got up, and he stood with her. "What if I could get you more shifts at the club? You must be on more bucks an hour there than at some crummy grocery store, and you wouldn't have to work your ass off to get it."

Her blood ran cold, and she tensed immediately.

"No, I can guess what I'd have to do with my ass to get it. No thank you. I'm not interested. Now if you wouldn't mind leaving I have things to do."

She stalked over to the door, handed him his jacket, and waited.

"I didn't mean…" he began.

"I don't care what you meant. I don't need a job from you. I can get my own thank you very much, and what if it *is* a crummy grocery store? At least it's honest." She spat the words at him, hurt and anger welling up inside her.

"Summer, I think it came out all wrong. I didn't mean to insult your efforts or you. I wasn't implying anything…"

"Good-bye." The door was open, and the frosty air

that gushed in matched the cold feeling in her body as she threw him out of her home.

Nathan sighed, but he seemed to realize she wasn't going to listen right now. Without another word he walked out into the dim light of dawn and climbed into his car.

Summer slammed the door before sliding down it and collapsing into a heap of miserable, angry tears.

Chapter Four

Summer didn't feel much better after she'd had a hot shower and changed her clothes. Although she was really tired, she promised herself a good rest once she got back from the interview, ready for tonight's shift at Collar and Cuffs.

The bus journey into town was long and boring, and she was afraid she was going to fall asleep and miss her stop. Instead she concentrated on how much money she could make if she got this job.

The hourly rate was only just over half what she was being paid at the club, but she had the chance of more hours so she would make up the money that way.

She smiled as she thought of how she would be able to pay her way, and after a couple of months she might be able to start making inroads into the huge debts that bastard had left her with.

She stared out of the window as the memories came

flooding back to her, and she almost thought she spotted him walking down the street. Putting it down to her own imagination she tried to put the thought to the back of her mind. After all, there were probably loads of scruffy, lanky, sandy-haired guys in the world, all with unshaven faces and dirty clothes.

Colin would have no business this far south anyway, she reasoned. She'd left him behind in West Palm Beach, stoned out of his mind and exhausted after beating the shit out of her because she refused to give him any more money.

She had only found out that morning that the bastard had taken out a credit card using her details, which he had maxed out to the tune of three thousand dollars. Three thousand dollars that she was now liable for.

When she had discovered it in his wallet his biggest worry was how she had dared "snoop" into his affairs. The fact that it had genuinely fallen out of the back pocket of his trousers when he was too high to care about it was, apparently, beside the point.

She had been so shocked by his latest trick that she had yelled at him, despite the fact he had been shooting up all night.

She was already working four jobs to try to keep the roof above their heads and pay off the debts he had landed them with. All the money she had given him to go and pay bills while she was at work had been injected up his arm.

Recently, she had also been threatened by some guy he owed money to because he had conveniently disappeared for a couple of days without paying for his last few shots.

Not having paid the electric bill wouldn't have been such a problem as she was never home long enough to use the stuff anyway, but Colin had been livid when he'd crawled home, shaking and throwing up, only to find there was no heating on in the apartment.

There was also no food because whatever she bought disappeared whenever he had a case of the munchies.

He'd seemed such a nice guy when she'd first met him. He'd been working on a building site and had been proud to have muscles on him like Popeye. She had found his strength admirable at the time, but once his contract finished and he was out of work they weren't much use to him.

He started hanging around bars during the day while she was at work, although he promised her he was out looking for a job.

That was how he had met up with Alex Ross. Alex was well known for having gotten rich on the backs of other people, but Colin was in awe of him. He soon started peddling drugs for Alex, who convinced him to give them a try himself.

Those muscles started coming in handy again when people owed Alex money. Summer soon felt the brunt of them too. Each time Colin wanted money she couldn't give him, out would come those fists.

She'd tried to leave him once before, but he had caught up with her and beaten the crap out of her. That was when she decided she needed a plan. She hadn't been able to go too far the last time because she needed to keep her jobs and she had a commitment to continue renting her apartment for another five months. That had given her five months to save her money, cut her ties, and plan her escape.

A lot of her clothes had already been stashed in a locker at the train station, along with the cash she'd managed to hide from the bastard, and the few precious pieces of her mother's jewelry that she'd managed to buy back after he'd stolen and pawned them. One night, while he slept, she'd made a run for it.

Cutting off her long, wavy locks came in a flash of inspiration after she had tried for the umpteenth time to hide them under a baseball cap to disguise her appearance. She had been sad to see her hair fall to the ground as she'd hacked at it with a pair of blunt scissors but figured it would be worth the price of her freedom.

The bus pulled up just down the road from the grocery store, and she got off feeling drained and low. It had started to rain, and she was glad she didn't have to walk too far.

"I've come for the interview," she told the young guy behind the counter. "Ms. Powell's expecting me."

"She's been delayed, but you can wait if you want," he said, unhelpfully.

Summer sighed and decided to have a look around

the store while she waited. The floor wasn't as clean as she would have liked, and the shelves looked like they needed a good wipe over. Some of the packets and cans actually had a layer of dust on them, and she realized from the lack of customers that goods probably didn't get a very fast turnaround in a place like this.

The young guy wasn't exactly friendly, and she wondered why customers would want to come here at all.

Over an hour later, Summer was beginning to get agitated. She had walked around the store several times by now and was sick of the sight of the place already.

"Do you know when she'll be here?" she asked the young guy.

He shrugged. "She doesn't tell me anything. I just work here."

"Do you have a number I could call her on?" she asked hopefully.

He shook his head.

"Well could I leave a note with you to explain that I was here but she's obviously not shown up, so I can come back tomorrow instead?"

He shrugged again, and she pulled out a scrap of paper and jotted down her message. She was just handing it to him when she heard someone clip-clopping across the tiled floor behind her.

"Summer, I'm so sorry to keep you waiting. Do come through." The woman didn't look very sorry, but Summer followed her through into the back of the store anyway.

"You've worked in a store before, you said, didn't you?" Ms. Powell began as she poured them each a cup of coffee from a machine in the corner.

"Yes. I've worked in a food store, a general store, and a hardware," Summer told her, eagerly taking the coffee from her.

"Good. And you're used to long hours then, I presume?" Ms. Powell sat behind a small desk and gestured for Summer to sit opposite.

It was rather a cluttered room, with stock piled high on shelves, and one corner turned into a sort of office. The whole place smelled of plastic, which Summer guessed must be from all the packaging. It was quite over-whelming.

"Yes," she concurred.

"Well, you need to be here for eight o'clock sharp. You can manage that?"

Summer nodded, but at the back of her mind seethed a bit over her boss's own tardiness.

"Good. Well, in that case, the job's yours." Ms. Powell looked like she had just handed over the crown jewels.

A quick "Thank you" was all Summer could muster. Why couldn't she have conducted the interview over the phone? Or just told her that yesterday?

"You'll find overalls on the back of that door." The middle-aged lady pointed. "You need to get that pallet-load on the store floor as quickly as you can, and don't forget to rotate the stock."

Summer was stunned. "You want me to start *now*?"

"There's no time like the present, dear." Ms. Powell looked like she had lost interest in her already and began flicking through the morning paper.

Summer felt a heavy thud in her stomach. She was looking forward to going home and getting some sleep before tonight's shift.

"I have to work tonight," Summer spluttered. "I start at six."

Ms. Powell looked over her glasses at her, frowning. "Oh, how inconvenient. You'll have to hurry then, won't you?"

Summer nodded dumbly. It was nearly eight o'clock, so she hoped that if she got the job done quickly she might just get home in time to get some rest before her shift at the restaurant. She hurriedly put on the overalls and set to work.

"You'll need to clean the shelves down before you load them up," Ms. Powell shouted after her as Summer took an armful of cans through the store.

Summer placed them on the floor next to the shelf and went back for a bucket and cloth.

"You can't leave food on the floor, stupid!" The young guy had managed to move from his seemingly permanent position behind the counter and poked his head through to the back of the store.

Summer seethed and looked over to the boss for some support. Ms. Powell looked up from the paper and tutted. "I thought you would have known better than that, dear. You *did* say you had worked with food before, didn't you?"

Summer opened her mouth to protest that the food on the floor was, in fact, canned, and would have been no different than being stacked on the wooden pallet in a dusty warehouse, but remembered how desperate she was to keep this job, so she said nothing.

She spent the next few hours cleaning the shelves before restocking and wiping the dust off the cans. She wasn't even halfway though emptying the massive pallet when Ms. Powell called through.

"Summer, you need to relieve Larry for his lunch now. You know how to use a cash register, don't you?"

"Yes, Ms. Powell."

Larry smirked at her and took off his overalls. He still had a customer waiting to be served in front of him, and Summer had a bucketful of water to dispose of before she could take over.

The young guy wasn't waiting around, though, and promptly left the store. Ms. Powell returned to the back room, and the customer huffed loudly.

"Is someone going to serve me or not?" he grumbled. Summer had the bucket in her hand and was heading toward the back of the store.

"Can I just..."

"No you cannot! Either you serve me now or I'll take my purchase elsewhere!" the man bellowed at her, and Summer turned bright red.

"What's the matter?" Ms. Powell suddenly appeared in front of her with an angry expression.

"I'm waiting to be served!" the man shouted.

"I was just..." Summer lifted up the bucket to show her boss what she was doing, but the woman obviously wasn't interested.

"The customer always comes first, Summer. You should know that. Now just leave what you're doing and serve the gentleman!" Her voice was sharp, and Summer felt herself go hot right through her body. She placed the bucket on the floor and went behind the counter.

After that she had a continuous stream of customers. She realized that lunchtime must be the busiest time for the store—although no one spent very much—and thought how convenient it was that Larry took his break when he did.

Luckily the cash register was the same type she had used before, so she was able to ring up the sales without any difficulty, although it seemed whoever had priced the goods was in the infuriating habit of placing the label over the bar code so they wouldn't scan properly.

Summer had to keep reminding herself this was just the means to an end, and the end result would be worth it. Anger boiled inside her though.

A fake smile covered her face, and she did her best to sound cheerful and friendly as one miserable customer after another trundled up to the counter, moaning at how long they had been kept waiting to be served.

Larry finally returned just over an hour later and

rushed into the store. He was speaking into his cell phone and looking at his watch as he hurried around to the back of the store.

Summer was still serving a customer when she heard an almighty clatter and Larry yelling as he tumbled to the floor, where he proceeded to slide in a puddle of dirty water.

"What on earth...?" Ms. Powell appeared in the doorway with a face like thunder.

"Who the fuck left that there? I think I've broken my leg!" Larry yelled angrily from his position on the floor.

Summer felt sick to her stomach as she finished serving the customer and then rushed over.

"What the hell did you leave that there for?" Ms. Powell screeched.

"You said..." Summer stopped herself short as she felt her face burning up with rage.

"I told you to leave it while you served *one* customer over an hour ago!" The lady screamed at her.

Every customer in the store turned and looked at Summer, who, for the third day in a row now, wished the floor would open up and swallow her whole. Anger and embarrassment roiled inside her. She had just about had enough.

"I have been serving customers ever since. I didn't get a chance to put it away because you told me to take over while he had his lunch." Summer spoke through gritted teeth, pointing at Larry, who had now managed to sit up but was holding his leg like an injured quarterback.

"Are you serving or not?" an old woman snapped from the counter.

Summer turned and glared at the woman.

"Well, serve the lady!" Ms. Powell shouted. "I'll call an ambulance for Larry, and you'll have to cover for him while he's not here."

An ambulance? She had to be kidding! As soon as Ms. Powell went into the back to use the phone, Larry shot Summer a smirk. Summer saw red. She hauled off her overalls and followed the woman into the back room.

"Yes, an ambulance. There's been an awful accident." Ms. Powell looked up in amazement when she saw Summer pick her way through the dirty water and up to the desk.

"Isn't anyone serving?" the old lady called through from the store.

"What do you think you're doing? Get back out there! You've got customers to serve and all this mess to clean up! And if that boy sues, *you'll* have to cover it, you know!" Ms. Powell's face was bright red as she hollered at Summer, while someone from the ambulance service could be heard asking for directions from the phone.

Summer calmly picked up her purse from the desk. "Correction. *You've* got customers to serve *and* a mess to clean up. And if that boy with nothing more than a bruise on his leg decides to sue, it will be *you* who will have to cover it!"

"You get back here this instant!" the woman hollered.

"Your store. Your staff. Your mess. Oh, and *your*

problem!" Summer's voice, as well as her expression, was as cool as an ice cube in winter as she waved her hand to the seething woman and carefully made her way through the stream of dirty water.

She couldn't resist giving Larry a smirk as he sat in the puddle gawping up at her as she left the store.

Chapter Five

It was just after four o'clock when Summer entered her tiny apartment. She picked up her mail and then sank into the sofa with a massive sigh. What a day.

She kicked off her shoes and curled up with her head on the arm of the couch. The events of the day whirled through her brain, and then the thoughts of last night sprang to mind.

Suddenly remembering she had to leave for work in just over an hour, she went into the bedroom and set her alarm clock. She allowed herself exactly one hour to sleep, and then she could quickly change and get to work on time. The bed looked so inviting she snuggled up straight away and laid her exhausted body on the soft bedspread.

The alarm was ringing after what felt like a few minutes, and she shot up and grabbed a quick shower, hoping it would wake her up.

She was glad she had such a short, easily manageable haircut now, and she briskly dried herself before applying a little makeup.

It was still raining outside, so she didn't bother to dry her hair and wore a pair of loose trousers with sneakers to walk to work. She pulled on a T-shirt and a waterproof jacket, stuffed a couple of unread letters in her pocket, and set off. She'd read the mail later.

Summer had hoped that the walk would wake her up a little, but she was wrong. The weight of the day, including her argument with Nathan this morning, hung heavy on her shoulders, and she was exhausted by the time she arrived. She felt like a drowned rat standing outside the club.

She noticed Nathan's car in the parking lot and sighed. She just hoped she wouldn't bump into him tonight. He would be bound to ask about the interview, and then he would probably laugh at her for putting in all those hours for no pay. She began to wonder if she had done the right thing in walking out the way she did, but she knew she couldn't handle any more of that shit. No siree. Her days of being dumped on like that were over.

"Are you OK?" Heaven asked when Summer arrived in the changing room.

"Just tired," Summer replied with a smile.

"Let's hope for a quiet night." Heaven closed her locker and headed for the bathroom, leaving Summer to change.

She sighed as she put on the heels. Her legs ached

already, but she was glad that she had worn flat shoes all day.

Checking herself out in the large mirrored wall, she noticed the dark rings under her eyes and wished she'd brought some makeup to cover them. Too late now.

"Good evening, everyone. We've got another busy service tonight. The soup is oxtail and the vegetables are shiitake mushrooms, roasted vine tomatoes, and snow peas. Everything is on tonight. Well, so far anyway." Dominic actually cracked a smile, and everyone tittered at his aside.

Summer felt that he was having a dig at her because of last night and felt herself getting hot. She glared at him. So much for his apology.

He looked up just then and seemed surprised by her reaction. "Summer, you're with Tuesday tonight, OK?"

She nodded.

Tuesday clapped her hands gleefully and smiled over at Summer, who smiled back. It was nice to feel wanted.

"All right, everyone, let's have a good service." Dominic finished the curtain call with a flourish, and everyone went to their stations.

"Are you all right?" Tuesday asked with a frown.

"Fine. Just tired, that's all." Summer shrugged and smiled. She loved Tuesday's thick Irish accent.

"When's your day off?" Tuesday opened the drawer and checked that everything was in order.

"Tomorrow." Summer sighed. Thank goodness she'd

decided against that job. If she had to work a whole day from eight o'clock tomorrow morning she'd be dead on her feet. And the thought of working for that awful woman with that obnoxious guy made her skin crawl. She shuddered.

"Any plans?" Tuesday handed her some napkins to fold.

"Sleep. I might just spend the whole day in bed." Summer smiled at the thought.

"Sounds great. I've got a dental appointment tomorrow afternoon. Having a tooth extracted. I hate the dentist," Tuesday said with a frown.

"I don't envy you." Summer grimaced.

Service was steady for a change, and Summer was able to concentrate on the job in hand instead of her aching limbs and her rotten life. Tuesday was a really cheerful companion, and they joked about some of the customers in hushed tones.

"People-watching is one of my favorite hobbies," Tuesday whispered as a man with a bad toupee sat at table thirty-one.

"I hope it's not windy tonight," Summer muttered.

Tuesday giggled. "I need to stop laughing. I have to take their menus over, and I just know they'll realize what I'm giggling over."

"Do it slowly," Summer said with a grin. "Any sudden draught and..."

"Summer." Dominic was suddenly right behind her.

Tuesday had a hand over her mouth still trying to stifle a laugh. Her expression was so comical that it made Summer want to giggle too, and she sucked her cheeks in hard to suppress it.

Summer took a deep breath before turning around to face the maître d'. She found him looking at her a little oddly and wondered if he had seen her with Nathan last night after all. The thought sobered her, and she flushed.

"Yes, Sir?"

Damn! She'd heard all the staff calling him that, and now she knew why. They obviously knew he was a Dom. Heck, they were probably all subs. Hadn't Hope said that only subs were allowed in the restaurant? Or was that the Bottom Bar? She frowned as she tried to recall, and then remembered that her boss was standing in front of her.

"I think table thirty-one needs menus," he said quietly.

"I'm on it," Tuesday piped up, taking the folders from the shelf of the dumbwaiter.

Dominic looked a little puzzled but nodded.

"Thank you." He turned to Summer. "We haven't got a sommelier again tonight. Darren Hall rang in sick again. Would you be willing to help out if anyone asks for advice?"

"Of course." She narrowed her eyes, not sure if he was having a dig at her for selling one of their most expensive wines last night.

"Thank you. I'll let you know if you're needed." He

walked away with her watching after him. He was a tough man to read.

Summer wondered if she was being paranoid, but if she wasn't that was the second jibe he'd had at her tonight. She was seriously beginning to wonder if he *had* seen her with Nathan last night and wasn't happy about it. After all, she was a member of his staff. Well, it wouldn't happen again.

"The expo's in a bad mood tonight," Tuesday confided when she'd finished serving table thirty-one their appetizers.

"That's all we need." Summer rolled her eyes and went to clear a deuce by the window.

It turned into a busy service, and Summer was rushed off her feet. Judy, the expo, was sure in a foul mood, and Summer frowned as she heard the young woman curse at April for taking too long picking up her order.

"Just get on with it," Judy snapped. "By the time you get it out there the food will be stone cold!"

Summer watched April flush. The black-haired waitress had been so kind to her yesterday, and she wasn't about to stand by and watch her be spoken to like that.

"Leave her alone. She's doing her best," Summer shouted down the line.

Even the clanging of pots and pans seemed to stop as everyone turned to look at her.

"What did you say?" Judy's face went bright red, and she clenched her jaw as she turned her mean little eyes on Summer.

"I said she's doing her best. Stop picking on her."

"How dare you speak to me like that? The maître d' will hear about this!" Judy spat the words out at Summer.

Summer felt herself go hot but wasn't sure whether it was embarrassment or just plain anger.

"Good. It's just a pity he didn't hear you being rude to the staff tonight." Summer wasn't going to back down now. Trying to save her job at the grocery store had led to being well and truly dumped on, and she was darned if she was going to let it happen here. Besides, April was her friend, and she wasn't going to let "Rudey Judy" or anyone else pick on her.

The head chef brought over the rest of April's order himself, and she took it with a whispered "thank you." The large man grinned, winked at April, and then studied Judy and Summer as if he was watching a tennis match.

"Table twenty-five entrées, please." Summer stared at Judy, daring her to be rude again.

Judy pursed her lips before requesting the order from the chef. "Twenty-five away please, chef."

The man grinned. "Coming up." He called the order, and the noise slowly resumed in the kitchen.

"Thank you." Summer gave her sweetest smile as she took the entrées into the restaurant.

"Thanks for sticking up for me. But she's bound to tell Master Dominic," April whispered when Summer passed her station.

"Let her." She shrugged. She really was past caring now.

Toward the end of service Summer noticed Dominic walking purposefully toward her. She felt a thud of dread in her stomach, guessing that Judy had been speaking to him.

"Summer." He beckoned her away from the table where she was setting up.

She braced herself.

"Table twenty-two are asking for champagne. Would you serve them, please?" His voice was low, and he looked a little wary as he spoke to her.

"Of course." She nodded and went over to fetch the wine list. She was aware of Dominic's eyes boring into her back as she went over to the small table and spoke to the guests.

As service came to an end there was an atmosphere of relief in the room. The girls quickly finished tidying their stations and re-laying the tables and then gathered for the debrief.

"Thank you everyone. Another busy service, but you all did incredibly well. Wine sales are up for the second night running, so well done." Dominic looked over at Summer, and Heaven gave her a friendly nudge.

"As it stands we should have a quieter night tomorrow, but all that could change, of course. It's a rough night out there so take care going home. Get some rest and I'll see some of you tomorrow."

A ripple of applause signaled the end of the shift, and the staff made their way to the door en masse.

"Summer, could I have a word, please?" Summer felt herself flush at Dominic's request.

She walked over to him, taking deep breaths to steady her nerves.

"I just wanted to know how you felt having finished your first week with us?" he began.

"Fine." Her teeth were as clenched as her fists while she braced herself for the worst.

He raised his eyebrows. "You look tired. Are you all right?"

She narrowed her eyes at him. She saw where this was going. "I'm tired so I was rude to Judy, I suppose?" she imagined smarting off. Instead she said, "I am tired. It's late. But I'm fine."

Dominic frowned. "Are you *sure* everything's all right?"

Summer sighed irritably, wishing he would just get to the point. "Everything's fine, thank you, Sir. I just had a busy shift, and now I'm ready to go home." Her voice was clipped.

Dominic pursed his lips. "I heard about your altercation with Judy earlier."

She looked up at him expectantly.

"Do you usually speak to the expeditor like that?" His eyebrows were raised and his voice was calm.

"No," she said, staring him in the face. "But then I've never worked with one who was so rude to the staff before." She felt herself go red but was glad she had kept the tremble out of her voice.

"I see." He took a deep breath, and she watched his change in stance as he seemed to loosen up a little.

"Excuse me, Sir." The bartender came across to inform Dominic there was a call for him.

"I'll take it now," Dominic replied. "Thank you for helping with the wine tonight, Summer. Great work. Have a good rest, and I'll see you next time." With that he hurried over to the bar, closely followed by the young bartender. Summer breathed a sigh of relief.

As she walked back to the changing room, she felt a little irked by his last comment and wasn't sure about his sincerity.

The room was empty as she quickly kicked off her heels and changed into her comfortable clothes. Something fell from her jacket as she pulled it from her locker, and she bent down to find the letters she had stuffed in her pocket earlier.

One envelope was obviously junk mail, but the other was handwritten. A cold shiver ran up her spine as she checked out the shaky scrawl. With trembling fingers she tore it open.

Hey bitch

Bet you thought I wouldn't find you—well you will have to do better than that! You owe me big time and I intend to collect my payment.

Do not think your fancy new friends can help you

either. One word to them or the cops and your new boss will find out all about you, slut!

I will see you soon. You can count on it!

Summer slammed the door of the locker shut. Her mind was racing, and her heart thumped painfully against her ribs.

"*Shit*!" She punched the locker door, hurting her fist in the process, but she didn't care. Angry tears rolled down her cheeks, and she felt herself flush.

"Are you OK?"

She spun around to see Nathan standing in the doorway, his suit jacket hooked on his finger above his shoulder, and his shirt half unbuttoned. He looked amazed at her and took a step into the changing room.

"No, actually I'm not OK. Happy?" She snarled at him, dismayed that he should see her in this state, annoyed that he should look so handsome.

Nathan walked toward her with his hands up in the surrender position. "Hey, I just came to see if you needed a ride home. It's awful out there." His voice was calm, which somehow made her feel more irate.

"No. I don't need your lift. I don't need your advice. I don't need anything from you. So just stay out of my life, OK?" she hollered.

He frowned. "You look tired. Have you had a bad day?" He looked concerned, but it only made matters worse.

"Yes, thanks. I've had a fucking awful day if you must know! I got taken for a ride when I went for that job you told me not to get. I only got one hour's sleep all day. That bitch in the kitchen nearly lost me my job. Then my fucking boss chewed me out all night. And now this! Yes, I think you can safely say I've had a bad day!" she yelled at him, taking a step backward as he came toward her.

"Now...what? What's happened?" He narrowed his eyes, and she realized she'd said too much. Angrily she screwed up the letters and thrust them back into her pocket.

"Never mind. Just get out of my way!" She stormed past him angrily and nearly bumped into Dominic right outside the door. She knew he had heard her rant from the expression on his face, but he didn't speak to her. He just stared.

Summer ran out of the building and into the dark, stormy night, which perfectly matched her mood.

She was drenched within minutes of leaving the club, but she didn't care. The cold seeped into her bones, and she wasn't sure if it was the weather or the shock.

Her blurry vision read every person on the street as a threat, and she ran as fast as she could to get away from there.

A large, silver car sidled up to her, and the window opened slowly. "Get in, Summer. This is stupid!" Nathan's voice called over.

"Fuck off!" She was sick of being called stupid. She was even sicker of people *thinking* she was stupid.

"Summer, wait. Something's not right. Let's talk about this."

"I've got nothing to say to you, asshole!"

A second later she heard the engine stop and turned to see him hurrying out of the car. She started to run again, but her head had turned to mush, spinning and aching, and she couldn't see straight. She felt two strong arms grab her just before everything turned black.

Chapter Six

Summer awoke in a luscious, soft bed with sunlight streaming in through a crack in the curtain. She sat up and looked around, dazed and confused.

"Hey, sugar." Nathan sat on the edge of the bed, placing a cup of hot coffee on the nightstand.

He looked even more gorgeous than ever dressed in a white shirt and Levis. As usual, his shirt buttons were partially undone, allowing an enticing shock of dark hair to peep through from his ripped chest.

She stared at him blankly, trying to fathom what was going on. She knew she should be angry with him, but it was hard when he looked so gorgeous and she felt so comfortable.

He grinned. "It's all right. Don't look so worried. You're at my place. I thought it best after you passed out in the street."

"W-what?"

"Did you miss your dinner again last night?" He had one eyebrow raised—it was the sexiest expression she had ever seen.

Her mind raced back to yesterday. Not only had she missed dinner—because she had chosen to get an hour's sleep before her shift, but also breakfast—because of her interview. Then, she realized, lunch too, because of that damn awful job. She wasn't about to tell him that though, so she just nodded.

"I thought as much." He shook his head, rolling his eyes. He placed a large, warm hand over hers. "You need a keeper," he told her with a grin.

More like a bodyguard. She snorted. Colin was on to her. He wouldn't look for her here though. Hopefully Nathan had bought her some thinking time by bringing her to his home. The thought eased her mind.

Summer smiled. She felt a little more relaxed now that she was warm, dry, and rested—and safe! She was also feeling a little embarrassed for her earlier barrage of abuse, although Nathan didn't seem at all perturbed.

"The bathroom's through there. Take a hot shower if you like. There's a robe behind the door. I'll get some breakfast on."

It was then she noticed that she was naked under those covers.

"Did you...?"

"Had my eyes closed the whole time, love." He

chuckled deep in his throat. "I won't take a peek until you clearly want me to." He gave her a wink before he left the room.

She couldn't help but be turned on a little.

Summer took a minute to really take in her surroundings as she sipped the aromatic coffee. The room was huge and tastefully decorated in cream with gold accents and dark, antique furniture. The huge bed was in the middle of the room with claw-footed night-stands either side and a large dressing table against one wall. The picture window took up a large portion of another wall, festooned with luxurious, long drapes.

Her feet sunk into the lush carpet as she padded over to the bathroom, which turned out to be larger than her living room.

Steam rose from the double shower as the hot water soothed her aching limbs. She moaned as she closed her eyes and enjoyed the soft bubbles deliciously massaging her body. It felt like she was a million miles away from Colin and all the worry he caused her. She knew she would have to deal with it all soon, but for now she resolved to take a break from all that and just enjoy being safe for a while.

She looked around for some jell and found the spicy fragrance Nathan used. With a secretive grin she took the bottle and smelled it. It was like being surrounded by the man himself.

As she stroked her body with the sensual liquid she

closed her eyes again, imagining it was his hands, not hers, rubbing and caressing her skin.

Her nipples puckered under her own ministrations, and that electric cable that attached a woman's breasts to her pussy was suddenly alive with power.

She teased herself by stroking her arms and her abdomen before venturing lower. She was surprised at how sensitive her skin felt as she breathed in the scent of the handsome man.

Her outer thighs trembled slightly as she touched them, and their inner counterparts screamed out for attention. She obliged, her eyes tightly shut as she neared her aching pussy.

She recalled the anticipation of the other night, when Nathan had smacked her butt, sending ricochets of heightened sensation through her quivering labial lips. Her little hard nub had vibrated against her inner lips, lifting her to sensational heights, the like of which she had never felt in her life before that night.

The thought of him consumed her as she gently stroked her lips and swiped the hard nub of her clit, as he had, and she leaned back against the cool, tiled wall as her orgasm swept through her whole body, causing an audible moan to escape her lips. Bright lights flashed in front of her eyes, and she was overwhelmed by an unsteadiness that had her plastering herself to the wall in order to keep upright.

The warmth that flooded her sated body was

delectable, and she heard herself giggle with contentment.

Still smiling, she quickly washed her hair before emerging. When she saw what awaited her after stepping from the shower, she cried out.

Nathan sat on the small stool in the bathroom, watching her. She immediately grabbed the robe from the back of the door and wrapped herself up like a parcel.

"What the hell are you doing?" she screeched, coming down to earth with a tremendous thud.

"I could ask you the same question." He looked serious and she felt her pussy clench, though she couldn't understand why. Still, she was finding it hard to be completely mad at him.

"You said I could take a shower!" Her eyes were wide as she snagged a small towel from the heated rail and ran it through her hair.

"I did," he concurred, standing up slowly. "I didn't, however, say anything about allowing you to climax in my shower." He cocked one eyebrow, and she was sure she had stopped breathing.

"W-what?"

She followed him out of the door and back into the bedroom.

"Come and eat." His voice was deep and made her pussy gush all over again. She couldn't understand why she felt so turned on by him. He was the one at fault here. Still, she followed.

"What about my clothes?" Her voice was a little shaky.

"Later." He didn't even turn around as he marched out of the room, and she followed him down the hall to where the smell of bacon and sausages filled the air of an enormous breakfast kitchen.

He gestured to the table made up for their meal, and she sat down in silence. The chair, although wooden, had a luxuriously soft cushion that molded to her shape as she sat down.

She watched him move effortlessly around the room, piling up their plates with bacon, eggs, sausages, tomatoes, baked beans, mushrooms, and even black pudding.

He put a plate in front of her, along with a rack of hot toast. She moaned as she smelled the food, and he poured her some coffee before sitting opposite her with his own meal.

"This is just like I had in London," she told him with a grateful smile, "except that they serve tea. I prefer coffee though."

He nodded. "I hope you like it."

"It's delicious." She savored every mouthful. It had been nearly four years since she had sat in a café in Chelsea, enjoying a full English breakfast. The taste and smell took her back there, and she closed her eyes momentarily as she remembered how good it was.

That had been a lovely vacation, and one that she would never forget.

"Why were you in London?" He sipped his coffee as he asked.

"I went on a vacation with my parents. It was fantastic. We saw all the sights, you know, Buckingham Palace, the Houses of Parliament, the Tower of London, which is actually several towers. Oh, and did you know that Big Ben is the bell *inside* the tower, not the tower itself? It was fascinating. We had tea at The Ritz too."

She felt herself get excited just recalling that wonderful time.

"I've been there," he nodded. "Did you take a boat ride up the Thames?"

"Yes." She smiled and leaned forward into the conversation.

"Would you like to work in a place like The Ritz?" He pushed his plate to one side as he drank his coffee.

"Oh yeah! I bet they have to put up with some fussy tourists though." She giggled. "Actually I had a job in a tearoom, not quite as posh as The Ritz, but it was real nice."

Nathan frowned. "While you were on vacation?"

She giggled, placing her empty cup on the table.

"Sort of. I'd gone out there with my parents, and while I was there I got chatting to the lady who owned the place and she offered me the job. I couldn't resist. She helped me get a work permit and I stayed over there when my folks came home." The thought caught her breath, and she felt herself flush.

"What happened?" His voice was gentle as he seemed to pick up on the change in her.

"They... um... they had an accident. Not long after they returned home they were hit by a drunk driver. Killed instantly." She felt tears well at the edges of her eyes, and she blinked them away furiously.

"I'm so sorry." His hand was over hers in an instant. She loved the feel of his warm strength.

"What about you? Were you on vacation?" she asked as brightly as she could.

"No such luck." He shook his head. "No, it was work, I'm afraid. Even that trip up the river was to schmooze a client."

"Very romantic," she said, half to herself.

He laughed. "Ha! It was a guy, actually. A very rich one at that. He wasn't at all impressed, either. I still never figured out why I had to entertain him over there, when he was about to be appointed in local government over here, but there you go."

Summer giggled.

"No, next time I go I want it to be a nice romantic break. Maybe with someone who knows their way around a little?" He looked at her conspiratorially, and she blushed.

"I'd love to go back to the Tower of London," she said eagerly. "Did you know that legend has it that if all the ravens flew away from it then the whole place would collapse?"

"No, I didn't." He looked surprised. She blushed, proud she had impressed him.

Summer stood up and started clearing away the plates.

"You don't have to do that here," he told her, taking them from her. "Go into the living room and sit down a minute. I need to talk to you."

She frowned but did as she was told.

The living room was as plush as the rest of the house. It was decorated in green and cream, again accented in gold. It appeared very restful, and she couldn't help curling up on the massive, soft sofa that almost filled one wall.

The central light fitting was not unlike the chandeliers back at the club, although not quite as ostentatious. The glass wall lights twinkled beautifully as the sun bounced off them and streamed in through the French windows occupying a whole wall.

At the far end of the room was an inglenook fireplace, which had horse brasses hanging over its walls. They too glinted in the sunlight.

The whole room was light and airy, and she loved its tranquility.

"Are you still tired?" Nathan walked in as she was lying on the sofa, thinking.

She quickly sat up. "No, I'm fine."

"That's good. You get real cranky when you're tired, did you know that?" He sat next to her with his arm casually resting along the back of the couch.

"I'm sorry. I was really rude yesterday. I didn't mean to be." She felt herself blush.

"Well, that's all right. What bothers me is how you got yourself into such a state. You're not eating or sleeping half enough. It's bound to affect your emotions."

Summer sighed. She knew he was right, but she really didn't need a lecture right now.

"Thank you for the breakfast, but I really need to be getting back now."

She went to stand up, but his arm immediately slid down to her shoulder, locking her in place.

"I haven't quite finished with you yet." He growled.

She felt her pussy tighten, and she stared at him. His eyes were darker than usual, and he had a very stern expression.

Summer felt her heart quicken, and she flushed.

"Oh?"

He sat facing her, still holding her in place.

"Now I know you've got a fiery temper on you, and Lord knows you can cuss a blue streak. But you see, as a submissive that kind of behavior is just not acceptable. Do you understand? Especially when it's aimed directly at your Dom."

Summer stared at him, open-mouthed. "What?"

"You heard me. Now I know you've been to BDSM clubs before, and you obviously know the protocol, which is why I was so disappointed in your behavior of late. I really didn't expect this from you, Summer."

He looked genuinely disappointed, and she felt a lurch in her gut. His voice was deep and did unholy things to her girly parts, and she couldn't understand why she felt so turned on while he was so clearly berating her.

"I'm sorry," she whispered.

"Well, I know you are, sugar," he told her. "But I think we need to figure out how we can avoid it happening again before we discuss your punishment, don't you?"

Summer felt a gush from her pussy at the mention of "punishment," though she knew it made no sense. Heat seared her body, and she trembled with excited anticipation. She nodded slowly, unable to speak.

"OK. Firstly you need to be eating regular meals. Now it shouldn't be that hard with your shifts at the club, but if it's a problem I can ask Master Dominic to arrange for you to have dinner before your shift starts?"

Summer was mortified. "No. I...I can manage that, thank you."

She was sure she saw a smirk twitch at his lips. "All right. But I'll be checking up on that, d'ya hear?"

"Yes, Sir." The response fell easily out of her mouth, taking her by surprise.

"Good. Now, what about sleep? You didn't actually take that awful job yesterday, did you?"

Summer wasn't sure whether it was a question or if he already knew the answer, but she shook her head anyway.

"That's good. You should listen to me, you know?"

She bit her lip and narrowed her eyes as she detected another smirk and debated whether to tell him that her decision wasn't in any way due to his suggestion but, on reflection, thought better of it.

Her mind wandered to that awful experience yesterday. It was all well and good sticking to her principles of not being taken advantage of, but she now still needed to find another job. He seemed to read her thoughts.

"Now, I've got a suggestion for you about a job, which you may or may not like, but hear me out anyway."

She frowned. "OK."

"Right, well, I noticed yesterday how good you are with figures, and you've obviously got a logical mind."

Her eyes narrowed.

"Now I know that the finance office at Collar and Cuffs is looking for a part-time clerk, and I wondered if it was something that might interest you."

Her heart leaped and her eyes widened. "But I haven't got any financial qualifications," she said quietly.

"That's all right. It's a clerk's job. Mainly filing and answering the phone, maybe dealing with simple queries. Cerys takes care of the day-to-day running of things. I'm sure she'd be more than happy to train you up if you're interested. It's only part time."

"That would be perfect, I could work around my shifts in the restaurant." She felt herself get hot with excitement. "Do you think I'd get it, though?"

"Well, you'd have to be real nice to the financial manager, who I hear can be a bit of a tough cookie at times. Think you could manage that?"

"Definitely. I can be nice. Real nice if I have to! What do I have to do? Is there a form or something?" She felt hope well inside her, and it made her quite dizzy.

He chuckled. "Slow down, sugar. I'm sure there'll be an interview or something, but you can handle that."

Summer nodded eagerly. "I can. I can handle anything I have to." That was the mantra she had been repeating to herself for the past four years. It had never let her down.

"Well now, I'm glad to hear that because there's the little matter of your punishment to discuss next."

Her mood changed in an instant. From elation she went to anticipation in a heartbeat. She swallowed hard, clenching her legs together as a trickle escaped her pussy.

"Punishment?" she whispered.

He nodded slowly as his eyes turned even darker.

"Now I know how much you enjoy a good spanking, but how about flogging, or a crop, maybe?"

Her pussy clenched and she stared at him. "I'm OK with a paddle and a flogger, and a crop if it's not too hard. And I've had a single tail," she told him, her voice a little shaky.

He raised his eyebrows. "Well now, that gives us some scope to work with."

Standing, he held out a hand to her. She took it and stood up, following him out of the room. Her heart was hammering, and she felt herself begin to pant with excitement.

He opened a door farther down the corridor, and she stared inside. Gone were the tranquil shades of the rest of the house. This room had black-and-red wallpaper and no windows.

A St. Andrew's Cross was attached to one wall, and a spanking horse stood in one corner. An antique-looking chest of drawers, holding heaven knows what delights, stood nearby, and an array of paddles, whips, and floggers hung on the wall above it.

A large bed took up one side of the room, with all manner of attachments to it, and something that looked a little like a surgical couch ominously stood near the middle of the room.

"You have your own dungeon?" Her voice wasn't much more than a whisper.

"I prefer to call it a playroom," he said with a smirk. "Come here."

She followed him over to the St. Andrew's Cross where he held a hand out for her robe. Slowly she removed it, and he hung it on a nearby hook. The cross, which was stored flat against the wall, was easily maneuverable, and he pulled it out so that it was accessible from both sides. Summer had been on one before and confidently climbed up before he fastened her wrists and ankles to the beams. With her back to him, she was now facing the wall and could see the assortment of instruments hung to one side.

"Look straight ahead," he ordered.

She diverted her eyes, taking a couple of soothing deep breaths as she felt his smooth hands run all over her arms, her back, and her legs.

"What's your safe word, Summer?" His voice held a deep, commanding tone, which stoked the fire in her belly even more.

"Banana, Sir."

"Good girl."

She hardly had time to bask in the delight of his response before she felt a hard "thwack" across her back.

"Aah!" she yelped as another five swats flailed her soft flesh in quick succession. Then came the warm caress of those large hands, and she sank deeper into the wooden cross.

Thwack. Thwack, thwack, thwack, thwack! The single tail stung and soothed all at the same time, and she moaned as his hand touched her again.

She was glad he hadn't asked her to count them out because she couldn't. She was soon lost in her own little world. One in which only they existed and pain morphed into pleasure in a delicious cocktail of fervor and delight.

Every now and then she was aware of his soft, deep voice, soothing her, checking on her and praising her. As she floated higher on her cloud of ecstasy she felt the burn in her stomach reach a crescendo, and she screamed his name in her release.

"Good girl. I'm so proud of you," he cooed as he

gently kissed her neck. Then he carefully unfastened the straps and carried her over to the large bed.

She wasn't sure when he had removed his clothes, but she looked up to see him standing over her, his eyes black with lust, his skin covered in a silken sheen of sweat. His monstrous manhood wept for attention, and she held her hands out to him. He quickly sheathed himself before kneeling on the bed, leaning over her panting body.

"I want you, Summer," he whispered, his hoarse voice barely audible.

"Yes," she breathed.

He pulled her knees out to the sides, opening up her dripping pussy for his delectation. She saw pure lust in his eyes as he gazed at her body, and in that moment nothing in the world mattered except for him.

His engorged cock kissed at her outer lips before tentatively probing deeper. She felt her body stretch to accommodate his massive size, and she moaned as he pulsed in and out of her, getting deeper with each thrust.

She screamed at the delicious sensation of being ripped in two as she welcomed him in up to his hilt. He paused for a second, and she relaxed while he took her mouth in a sensual, heated kiss.

The warmth of his body enveloped her, and the gorgeous soft hairs of his muscular chest tickled her breasts, tantalizing them before his hands stroked her face, her throat, and then her hard, tightened nipples.

She squeezed her eyes tightly shut as she savored every sensation his incredible form bestowed on her.

The fire raged through her body once more, and his ardor increased as he plunged in and out of her soaking pussy, sending exquisite tremors right through her heated body.

"Look at me," he urged, and she opened her eyes to see his huge, black pupils boring into her, reflecting the desperation tearing through him.

That inexplicable look in his eyes, the rasping sound of his voice, the glorious feel of his cock—all of it—sent her plummeting over the edge.

She screamed as she stared into his beautiful, contorted face, only to be rewarded with his guttural roar as he shot his load into the waiting condom. Bright silver lights filled her peripheral vision while he filled her mind, body, and soul.

In that instant Summer loved that man and hated the sack that deprived her of his seed. It didn't make sense, she knew that, but then, none of this did.

His hot body slumped to one side of her, and she snuggled in close to his skin. His strong arm came around her, holding her right where she wanted to be.

They both panted, gasping for the same air as their sated bodies gradually calmed and relaxed. Summer closed her eyes and drifted into the most peaceful sleep of her life.

. . .

Nathan lay quietly while the sleeping beauty in his arms snuggled even closer to him, sighing with contentment. Her face glowed and she was smiling. He felt warmth inside him like he had never felt before. Not even when he and Sharon had made love. Love.

There it was.

The way she had quickly accepted him calling her his sub and he her Dom had astonished him. She had looked shocked at first but hadn't voiced any objection.

The way her face shone when she had heard about the possibility of the finance job—the job that *he* would make possible.

He smiled at the satisfaction of knowing he was actually able to do something to help his vulnerable, proud sub. Of course she would explode all over again when she realized who the finance manager was, but, in a way, he would look forward to it.

He would have to go to the club later to put the wheels in motion, but he knew it wouldn't be a problem.

His eyes fell on the St. Andrew's Cross, and he recalled the vision of beauty as she stood there, completely naked, open to him. The sound of her yelp when he had first used the single tail on that delectable, soft back of hers had nearly ripped his heart out. He knew he hadn't hit her hard, but what was hard for her? He didn't really know. All he did know was that she had needed it as much as he had.

After spanking her the other night he had desperately wanted to take her there and then in the club. But it wouldn't have been right. She needed to know first that she could trust him. And with his boss as well as hers just across the bar from them it would have felt awkward afterward for all of them.

Even still, he had needed to yank himself off twice in the shower when he got home just to enable his jeans to fasten.

He looked down at her. She looked so serene now, quite the opposite of earlier.

Her passion had been palpable when she was on that cross, and again here, on the bed. When she had stared at him while their orgasms overtook them, he had seen something he had never seen before. He knew she was beautiful, but that look was something much more...*more*.

The intensity, the wonder in her face when she had looked at him was inexplicable.

The way she clung to him now made his heart melt. His little sub needed him, and that was a great feeling. Now all he had to do was convince her to accept his help.

He covered her with a thin blanket as he watched her sleep. He must have dozed off for a while because he woke to feel her moving.

"Sorry, I didn't mean to wake you," she murmured, sitting up.

"It's fine, sugar. Are you OK?"

"Yes. I just need the bathroom, that's all." She looked a little sheepish, and he kissed her cute little face.

He got up with her, and while she used the bathroom he made some coffee.

Hearing the shower running, he took both cups through with him. He was surprised to hear her humming while she washed, and he sat on the little stool and watched her as he had before. She was smiling as she helped herself to his jell again, and he wondered what she was thinking about.

Her hands didn't linger on her body this time; it was strictly a utilitarian event. She switched off the water with a sigh and turned around.

"Have you been watching me again?" She wasn't shocked this time, just smiling although obviously a little surprised.

"Yes. Is that a problem?" He winked at her and was rewarded with that tinkling laugh of hers that touched his very heart.

She shook her head, grabbing a towel. "No, Sir. You can do whatever you want." She gave him a salacious look up and down, and he chuckled.

"I wish I could, sugar, but some of us have work to do."

He took the towel from her and rubbed her dry, taking extra care of her red, striped back. "How are you feeling?" he murmured in her ear while he wrapped a dry towel around her.

"Great." She nodded and smiled. "That was totally awesome."

"*You* are totally awesome," he told her and watched her blush.

"How are you?" Her big eyes looked up at him through her long, black lashes, and his heart melted again. She looked genuinely concerned.

"I'm great," he assured her, kissing the top of her head.

She smiled and went to the door. "Where are my clothes?"

"You want to get dressed?"

She giggled. "Of course. I need to go home. And you need to get to work, remember?"

He felt a thud in his stomach. Soon she would be going back to that poky little apartment in one of the worst parts of town, and there was nothing he could do about it. He longed to tell her to stay here with him—to move in—but he knew that she wouldn't want that. Not yet, anyway. She was a proud woman, and he was proud of her.

"I'll get them. I put them in the dryer."

"Thank you. That was real nice of you," she said as he crossed the bedroom.

He noticed she seemed far more relaxed now. It was probably partially down to her having had such a good sleep, but he hoped it was something else too.

He gave her the dry clothes and hopped into the shower while she dressed.

The hot water soothed his aching back. He hadn't used the single tail in a while, and he had forgotten how much he had to exert himself when he used it. He'd released a lot of tension today, and he felt the world of difference in his body.

He tried to remember the last time he'd had sex but couldn't. Since Sharon had left him he had only taken the odd sub at Collar and Cuffs, but nothing meaningful or intense. Nothing like this.

He pulled on a pair of suit trousers and a cotton shirt, but didn't bother with a tie or jacket. He wasn't planning to be there for long.

"Have you got plans for tonight?" he asked her as she ran her hands through her hair, causing the top to spike up.

"It's my night off. I thought I'd be sleeping around the clock, but I'm wide awake now. I might just catch up on some reading."

"What about food?"

"What?" She frowned.

"You had a late breakfast. If you were in London you'd be having afternoon tea around about now. Surely you must be getting hungry? What about dinner?"

"I'm not hungry. Maybe I'll get something later." She shrugged. He guessed that in her blissful state she couldn't be bothered worrying about food, or anything else for that matter.

He sighed, unconvinced. "You'll eat now and then again later." He used his Dom voice, and she stared up at him in surprise.

Nathan went through to the kitchen and filled a

couple of baguettes with cream cheese and salad. He made some fresh coffee and looked around to find her studying him carefully. He wondered whether she actually had any food at home but couldn't exactly ask.

"Sit," he told her as he carried the tray over to the table.

She grinned as she complied, and she eagerly tucked in.

"I'll pick you up at seven tonight," he told her as they ate. "We'll go for a ride down to a little place I know by the river. They do wonderful food, you'll love it. Then we'll spend a couple of hours just chilling before I bring you back here. You'll need to get some stuff for staying over." He had it all worked out.

Summer stared at him. "What do you mean?"

He casually took another bite of his baguette.

"What don't you understand, sugar?"

She narrowed her eyes in thought. "You want to take me out to dinner?"

"Unless you've got other plans?"

"No."

"Great. I'll run you back to your place where you can collect your overnight stuff and have a read of that book you were talking about, and then I'll pick you up again at around seven. Is that OK?"

He frowned, a little concerned that maybe she didn't want to go out with him tonight.

If he had read her right that wasn't the case at all. She seemed quite content spending time with him, and he loved her company.

Summer smiled and nodded eagerly. "That would be lovely. I'd love to come. Thank you."

He sighed in relief.

As soon as they'd finished and tidied away their dishes, Nathan grabbed his keys. He really didn't want to break up such a wonderful day, but he knew Roland Dexter would be wondering where he was, and he could use the opportunity to set things up for the new clerk.

Summer looked radiant as he drove her back to her apartment. She was chatting about what a wonderful time she'd had and how hopeful she was about the clerk's position.

"I'll see if I can find out a little more about it tonight," he promised as they drew up outside her place. "Do you want me to walk you in?"

Summer giggled. "Nathan, it's only four thirty. I'm sure I can take it from here," she assured him, grabbing her jacket.

He leaned in and gave her a long, warm kiss on that luscious mouth of hers and watched as she walked over and let herself into the building. She waved and went inside so he set off for the club.

He would have a word with Cerys to see if she could draw up a list of duties that she could use some help with. In fairness, they had talked about getting in an extra pair of hands on several occasions, but somehow there always seemed to be other priorities. Now Summer was his priority.

He pulled up outside the club. It was quiet in the parking lot as the evening staff hadn't arrived yet, and most of the day staff had already left.

As he was getting out he noticed a piece of paper on the passenger chair. Thinking that Summer must have dropped something he reached over and took a look. He unfolded the note to see if it was anything urgent, and his heart fell into his boots.

Chapter Seven

When Summer had woken in Nathan Faulkner's arms she'd felt like she had died and gone to heaven. His heat, his scent and his body had surrounded her, concealing her in a safe cocoon she'd never wanted to leave. Except to pee. She'd badly needed to pee. *Damn.* She'd tried to creep off the bed without disturbing him, but he'd woken in an instant.

He hadn't seemed at all bothered at having to get up, and after relieving herself she'd taken the liberty of having a quick shower. It seemed a shame to wash the man off her, but at least she'd gotten to use his scented shower jell once more.

She smelled her arms now as she waved good-bye to him in her doorway. He was so handsome, and she couldn't get over the excitement in her stomach, knowing that he was going to be back in just a couple of hours.

She'd been shocked when he'd announced he had to work today. Having the day off herself, she had forgotten that not everyone was so lucky.

He was so confident and masterful. She loved the way he had worked everything out for her. Eat, home, then out again at seven and he even planned that she would stay with him tonight so she would know to get her things together. He was very organized, a trait that she was proud of in herself and loved in other people.

She let herself into the apartment, humming a country song. She felt lighthearted and so happy. Happier than she had ever felt. She knew they had only just met, but somehow she just felt that he was perfect for her.

She had never known anyone like him. The Doms she had met at the clubs in Daytona Beach were great for a few hours, but she never got emotionally involved with them. They made it clear that a relationship was not on the cards, and she couldn't imagine spending quality time with any of them outside of the dungeon.

She threw her purse on the sofa and went to the kitchenette for a glass of water. She was pleased that she had eaten today, as she had no food in the apartment. She was waiting for her next pay check before she could stock up a little but had so many debts to pay that she wouldn't be able to buy a lot.

She wondered whether Nathan had guessed that

much when he had offered the baguette. He certainly hadn't let on if he had, and she was grateful for that. She hugged herself, his scent wafting around her.

With a couple of hours to spare, Summer decided to pack her things together for tonight and then curl up with a good book for a while.

Her plan for today, apart from sleeping, had been to look for another job, but thanks to her knight in shining armor that wasn't a problem anymore. She smiled as she recalled how he had worked that all out too.

Giggling to herself, she wandered into the bedroom to gather her things. A cold chill ran down her spine as she entered the room, and she immediately felt that something was off. She had only taken one step into the room when the door slammed shut behind her.

"What time do you call this, whore?"

She felt the blood drain from her face as she turned around to see Colin staring menacingly at her from behind the door.

Although he still looked as stocky and strong as ever, his long hair was lank and greasy. His big eyes that she had once found endearing were now bloodshot with bags under them. He was unshaven and his clothes were dirty, adding to his scruffy appearance, and he smelled of stale sweat.

Fear and anger flooded her in equal measures, and she just stood trembling for a few seconds.

The glass of water in her hand was only half full, but

she splashed it into his face and then reached past him for the door handle.

"Bitch!" He was too fast and grabbed her arm.

"You've been out with your pimp again, haven't you? What in hell do you think you're playing at? You're coming home and you're going to sort this whole mess out, do you hear me?"

He yelled straight into her ear, one of his meanest tricks since he knew that she suffered badly from earaches, and she tried to smash the glass on his head.

Unfortunately he saw it coming, grabbed it out of her hand, and swiped it hard against her arm, causing it to shatter.

"Have a taste of your own medicine, bitch. Now you can see what it feels like!" he snarled at her as blood poured from her searing limb.

Summer screamed as his force pushed her backward and she landed on the bed. Blood dripped onto the white bedspread as he towered over her, evil in his eyes and the strength of a desperate man evident in his stance.

"What the hell do you want?" she screamed at him as indignant rage overtook her.

"You, bitch! You owe me and you know it!" His rancid breath made her retch as his face almost touched hers, his filthy hands sullying the pristine bed linen at either side of her flushed face.

"And just how do you figure that?" She spat the words at him.

"You left me in so much shit! You were supposed to

pay Ross off. When you didn't, he came after *me*. You've got no idea the trouble you've caused disappearing like that!"

"I don't owe him anything! I don't even know the bastard. If you owe him money that's your problem, sucker!"

She hitched her knee hard into his balls, and he crumpled like a leaf in autumn. Summer shot up and threw open the bedroom door, only to come face to face with one of Colin's cronies.

"Get her!" Colin choked.

The sneer on his face told Summer that there was nothing he'd like more, and he grabbed at her with grubby hands. She screamed and tried to fight back, but this guy was even bigger than Colin, and he held her in a vise-like grip.

"Come on, let's go!" Colin was on his feet now and grabbed her short hair in his fist.

Pain throbbed through her head, and her scalp stung. Her mind raced as she was dragged through her own lounge and out the door.

A pickup was chugging away just outside the main door to the apartment block, and Summer quickly looked around for any sign of Nathan.

"Don't even think about it, bitch!" Colin sneered at her as he opened the door and threw her onto the bench seat. He quickly clambered in next to her, and she was trapped between him and the driver.

Colin's henchman, Harrison if she remembered him correctly, climbed into the back.

The guy at the wheel, whom she didn't recognize, smelled of stale beer. Her heart pounded with dread as he whizzed the truck around and headed out of town at a speed that made her head spin.

"Where to?" the driver asked in a gruff voice.

"Ross is expecting her." Colin's voice was triumphant, and Summer felt the urge to slap him, but he had hold of her wrists.

"She got the money?"

"It doesn't matter if she hasn't. He's agreed to take the payment in other ways if she can't pay up."

Both men chortled, and Summer felt herself go boiling hot.

"We can always pocket the cash, and he can still take his payment." Harrison passed her wallet through the open window.

"Good man." Colin took both her wrists in one hand so he could open it.

"Her wallet was in her purse, just lying there on the couch. It was too good an opportunity to miss," Harrison explained proudly.

"I haven't got any money." she snapped at him. Luckily she hadn't been paid yet so she really was broke.

Colin held up her bank card. "You've got an overdraft, don't ya?" He sneered. "Once we're out of this dump we'll find a bank and see what we can get."

The driver guffawed, and the sound of Harrison

chuckling in the background could be heard over the revs of the old engine.

Summer considered telling them that the overdraft was already maxed out but then thought better of it. Anything that would delay their escape had to be a good thing, and she could waste a few minutes at a cash point if nothing else.

"Hey, maybe we can get some food. I'm starving." The driver sounded hopeful.

"You're always fucking starving, Mickey." Harrison called from behind them.

"Hey, don't knock it. I've got a case of the munchies too." Colin tucked her wallet into his breast pocket and rubbed his stomach. He was wearing a long-sleeved checked shirt, as usual, and Summer guessed his arms must be in a worse state than ever by now.

Her mind whirled while she studied the driver. He was a little older than the other two men, probably getting on for forty, Summer surmised. He had greasy Afro curls and coppery skin. Like the others, he was unshaven, and his beard looked like it still had the remnants of his last meal stuck in it. His moustache draped over his top lip, and she watched him chew on the corner of it. He had a filthy T-shirt and jeans on, and he smelled of sweat as well as the booze she had noticed when she first encountered him. He couldn't drive for shit, and the car swerved all over the road.

She quickly diverted her eyes when he noticed her staring at him and heard his leering chuckle.

Summer was glad both windows were open as the stench in that cab was literally making her stomach roil.

She didn't recognize the area they were whizzing through, having not been in Miami long enough to do any exploring yet.

"Bet you thought that ugly haircut would be a good disguise, did you? Or did your pimp insist on it?" Colin's sneer cut into her thoughts as sharply as his filthy nails were cutting into her wrists.

She glanced over at him with a look of disdain. He obviously took exception to her expression, as he used his free hand to slap her hard across the face. It stung, but it was something she was well used to from him.

"Don't you like it?" Her teeth were gritted and her jaw tense as anger welled from her stomach.

"You looked hideous enough before—you just look completely grotesque now." He jeered at her.

"So why were you with me for so long? Couldn't you get a pretty girl with your looks?" She couldn't resist the jibe and felt that the slap across the side of the head she received in return was almost worth it. She had become so accustomed to his violent outbursts she hardly felt the pain anymore.

The only thing that was really giving her grief right now was the arm that appeared to still have some glass stuck in it. Blood was still oozing onto her trousers where she had laid her throbbing limb, but at least she knew the material was clean. Goodness knows what infections she would catch from any of Colin's clothes.

"Why do you think, bitch? It certainly wasn't your looks. Why else do you think I had to get drunk or stoned just to bang you? And don't think you were my only meal ticket either. I've got plenty more dotted around the place, same as the rest of Ross's men. In fact I hear you've met one of their bitches already down here."

"I don't know anyone," she told him, wondering how he had found her. She knew Ross was a powerful crook and could well have connections down in Miami. If Colin had convinced him she would pay off his debts, it was just possible he might have put word out to find her.

"That's where you're wrong, slut," he snapped at her triumphantly. "A lot of people work at that posh club of yours, and word soon gets around about a newcomer. You women just love to talk, don't you? Luckily, Ross likes to listen."

Summer frowned. "One of the staff?"

"Yep. I guess you just thought they were all real friendly, didn't you?" He sneered.

"But how would you know anyone from there?"

"I don't. Someone who knows Ross fucks one of them now and then. Happened to mention that his woman came home yakking about a new girl who'd just started there, and Ross did the math. I'd already given him a rundown of all your 'talents' so it didn't take a genius to figure it out."

"So I see." She braced herself for the fist, which came flying at her cheek.

Her face throbbed as much as her head, and she sank back against the rock-hard headrest. It was difficult to think that someone at the club had given her away, they were all so nice to her. Except for Rudey Judy, of course. Although if it had just been pillow talk, it could have been quite innocent. One of her friends could easily have mentioned her without realizing the danger they were putting her in.

It was beginning to get dark, and she wondered what the time was. Nathan would surely have gone to the apartment to fetch her by now. What would he think when she wasn't there? Would he just knock on the door, get no answer, and assume she'd changed her mind? Would he just go home and forget all about her? The thought made her stomach churn and her heart ache.

No. That look in his eyes when they made love this morning told her that he wouldn't just forget about her. She had meant something to him. She just knew it. He had been so kind to her and took such good care of her that she knew he would be worried.

Would he get into her place? He would certainly be concerned if he went in and found her gone.

She closed her eyes imagining that gorgeous face of his, the feel of his touch, the scent of him. She bowed her head slightly and tried to breathe in the residue of his shower jell on her skin. Although faint, the aroma gave her strength.

He was her only hope now. No matter what, she'd find a way to survive until he came through.

Chapter Eight

Nathan got right back into his car and tore out of the parking lot.

On his way back to Summer's apartment he used his hands-free to call Dominic, just in case he'd had any news about her previous employment or even knew anything about her past relationship. He hadn't heard anything. *Damn!*

Dominic was concerned when he told him that something was wrong and she was in some kind of danger and promised to meet him at her place as soon as he could. That was some favor for a workaholic like Dominic. He never took time off work unless he really had to.

As he had expected there was no answer at the door, so he gave it a good kick and it opened. He cursed himself for not checking on her security before he had left her here.

Her purse sat on the sofa and he quickly checked it. Her wallet was gone.

The bedroom door was wide open, and he noticed scuff marks on the doorjamb. *Fuck.* The blood all over the sheets confirmed his fears.

He went next door, hammering hard with his fist until a middle-aged woman opened up.

"The girl next door. Something's happened to her. Did you hear anything?" There wasn't time for niceties.

She looked a little embarrassed. "Well, there was some screaming and banging noises, but I didn't know if that was her normal behavior. She only just moved in, you see..."

"Did you call the cops?"

"No." She blushed with shame.

"Does the CCTV work here?"

"Sometimes. There's an office..." She pointed to what looked like a cupboard door farther down the corridor, and he shot off in that direction, thanking her as he went.

He banged hard on the door she had indicated.

"Nathan?" Dominic's voice echoed in the corridor while Nathan waited for an answer.

"Down here."

Dominic ran toward Nathan just as a young guy opened the door in front of him.

"We need to check your CCTV right away. Something happened to the young girl from 104, possibly within the last hour. Did you notice anything?"

The open newspaper in front of the monitor told

him the answer to that one, and he pushed past the guy to get into the room.

"Hey, you can't just..."

"I think you'll find I just did, kid."

"Only the cops get access to those tapes," the guy protested, following Nathan over to the desk.

"You can call them if you want to. Meanwhile, show me the outside of the building on here." Nathan wasn't waiting around, and he soon felt Dominic at his elbow.

"She's been hurt." Nathan told him without looking up from the screen in front of him.

"I saw the blood." Looked like Dominic had been in her room too.

The young guy rewound the tape, and they stared at the entrance of the building as he slowly forwarded the tape again.

"Who's that?" Nathan pointed to the screen where a rusty old pickup had pulled up, the engine still running. A scruffy guy leaned out of the driver's window while his colleagues ran into the building.

"Never seen them before." The young guy shrugged.

Nathan was already jotting down the vehicle registration when he saw the guy coming back out of the main entrance, dragging Summer with him. Blood was gushing from her arm, and she was struggling in his massive grip.

Another guy was rushing out behind them, and they watched as the gorgeous blonde was shoved into the truck, which then sped off.

"Fifty minutes ago," Dominic announced, checking the time on the screen against his Rolex.

"*Damn!*"

"I'll call Steve." Dominic got straight onto his cell phone and was soon speaking to Steve Ratner, one of the dungeon monitors from Collar and Cuffs, who also happened to be a cop.

"Thanks for your help, kid," Nathan said to the young guy as he followed Dominic out of the office.

"He's running the plate right now. Your car or mine?" Dominic asked quietly, covering the mouthpiece of the phone.

"Mine." Nathan had left his car right outside the building, so he would have had to move it anyhow. He hadn't parked it properly earlier because it would have wasted too much time.

Besides that, he knew that driving would be more therapeutic for him than sitting in the passenger seat worrying helplessly.

They jumped in and sped off, with Dominic taking instruction from Detective Sgt. Ratner. It turned out that the pickup had put a lot of distance between them already, but once Nathan explained about the note, Steve confirmed that there would be a few squad cars on their trail now too.

"Do we know who this guy is?" Dominic asked.

"Nope." Nathan seethed. He hated secrets, especially since Sharon's little escapades.

"You really like her, don't you?" Dominic was a shrewd man and knew his friends well.

"Yeah. I like her a hell of a lot," Nathan admitted. "That's what makes this so fucking awful. I didn't know she was in trouble. I guessed she was in some financial strife but nothing like this. How did I not know?"

"You haven't known her long," Dominic reminded him.

"Yeah, but even so. I guess I knew there was more to her move here than she was letting on. Fort Lauderdale's where she'd come from, right?"

Dominic frowned. "Her last job was in West Palm Beach. Some club, but I can't get much out of them. She worked in Fort Lauderdale before that, as a silver service waitress, among other things. They gave her a great reference, said they were sorry to see her go. Some family problem or something meant she had to move."

Nathan felt his gut wrench. She hadn't lied to him, but it seemed there was a lot she hadn't told him.

"I wonder what it is the bastard thinks he's going to tell you that will make a difference," Nathan mused, handing him the note.

Dominic shook his head. "She's a damn good worker. I can't think of anything that would jeopardize her job, if that's what he means. Actually, she's the best we've got in the alcoholic beverages department. I'm considering her for the job of sommelier. The one I've got takes more sick leave than the rest of the staff put together, and anyone who can talk Brad Dexter out of his cash is worth their weight in gold, in my book."

"Yeah, I liked that." Nathan felt a sense of pride, and a smirk crossed his lips as they sped away from town.

"She went on to sell our most expensive bottle of Cristal the following night," Dominic said with a grin.

"That's my girl." Despite the seriousness of the current situation, Nathan found his face split into a shit-eating grin. This girl would be a great addition to the finance department.

"We've got a lead. Someone tried to use Summer's bank card in Medley." Steve Ratner's voice came over Dominic's cell, giving details of the latest whereabouts of the truck.

"We're onto it," Dominic confirmed as they swung a tight right and sped off down a back road.

"Let's get these bastards." Nathan felt the excitement bubble up inside him as anger and anxiety fought for pole position in his system, promptly knocking pride clean off first place.

Summer badly wanted to close her eyes as the throbbing in her head continued to pound. She needed to keep her wits about her, however, and thought it would be best to get some idea of her whereabouts just in case she got the opportunity to run. She made mental notes of key signs and places of interest—or at least those that stood out in her mind—as they sped carelessly down the back streets of goodness-knows-where.

"There's a small town down here where we can use the bank," the driver, who was apparently called Mickey, said with a smirk.

"OK, but we'll have to be quick. It's too risky to be here for long." Colin was starting to shake, and Summer guessed he was about ready for his next fix.

Mickey pulled over, and Colin leaped out of the car. Summer went to follow him out, but Mickey grabbed hold of her.

"It's all right. I know the number." Colin smirked at her, and she felt herself go hot. She had already changed her bank card number four times because she suspected him of taking money from her account but didn't realize he'd found it out again already. She wondered if she'd ever feel truly safe again, even if she got away.

"You're with me," Mickey sneered, holding her even tighter as Colin slammed the door shut.

She watched Colin pull her wallet from his pocket as he approached the machine.

"Never mind him, we've got a couple of minutes to ourselves." Mickey showed her a toothless grin, which made her feel sick.

Holding her with one hand, he put the other straight onto her breast, and she yelped at the shock. He squeezed it tight, a salacious expression on his pug-ugly face. Instinctively, Summer brought her leg up and kicked him before scrabbling over the seat and pushing the door open.

"Fuck you!" Mickey yelled, and Summer jumped out of the truck just as Colin finished at the machine and Harrison appeared in front of her, seizing her arms in his filthy hands.

"Nice try, slut," Harrison jeered at her, and she wriggled as much as she could. It was no good. The guy was a bulldozer.

"Get back in there, bitch." Colin punched her bleeding arm, and the agony that shot through her body was unbearable. Summer honestly thought she was about to pass out with the pain, but she wasn't so lucky. She heard her own scream as if she was listening from elsewhere, and she swallowed a mouthful of bile.

Harrison threw her into the cab, and Colin climbed in after her.

"Fucking whore!" Mickey slapped her face as soon as she got near him. "Think you can kick me and get away with it, do ya?"

Summer was aware of tears streaming down her face, and she sat still and quiet while they both subjected her to a barrage of abuse before zooming off down the road.

"Ten lousy dollars! Is that all you're worth?" Colin snapped at her, holding a note up in his grubby hand.

"You'll have to do a lot better than that when Ross gets hold of you," Mickey jeered with an evil laugh.

"I'm not waiting until then. You promised me my

share, don't forget!" Harrison hollered from behind them, and Summer felt a thud in the pit of her stomach.

"We'll all get our share before he does," Colin promised, giving her a sneer. "And you better make sure we all enjoy it."

She glared at Colin. "I thought you didn't think I was pretty enough for you?" she snapped.

"Ha! You've never been pretty, bitch, but that's never stopped me from boning you before, has it? With that fucking awful haircut I'll have to keep my eyes well and truly shut this time, or I'll think I've turned into a faggot. What in hell did you get it done like that for? At least when it was long it covered up that ugly fat face of yours." He laughed at her cruelly as hot tears streamed down her throbbing face.

Nathan likes it, she told herself. He said she was cute, and he ran his hands through it all the time when they made love that morning.

"I hope you like it up the ass, whore," Mickey joined in.

"We having a foursome?" Harrison yelled through the window.

"Might have to." Colin glanced at his watch, and Summer took the opportunity to check the time. It was nearly nine o'clock and was almost pitch dark outside. She wondered where Nathan would be right now, and her heart pounded. He was her hero. He would save her. She just knew it.

"Do they know, at that fancy club you work at, that

you're a hooker?" Colin sneered, and she knew that he was trying to quash any hope she might have left.

She seethed at his remark and then remembered that he had threatened to tell her boss all about her in his note. What the heck would they think? Would Nathan still want her?

"I'm not a hooker," she bit back.

"Yeah, right! You think I don't know how you made your money? Fuck, that's the only reason I stayed with you, you fat slut."

"She's good for something, then, eh?" Mickey piped up.

"Good enough for keeping a roof over your head and food in your belly. Oh, and let's not forget paying your fucking drug debts!" Summer had just about had enough. She knew that Colin and his friends could kill her. Even if they didn't, they would make damn sure Nathan wouldn't want her anymore. After they'd finished with her no man would ever want her again, and there wasn't a damn thing she could do about it. The thought made her feel physically sick, and she swallowed another mouthful of burning bile.

"He'll be at the meet point in half an hour." Harrison yelled from the back of the truck. He had evidently been on his cell.

"That doesn't give us long to have our fun!" Mickey groaned.

"Well if you step on it we might do it," Colin snapped.

Summer was beginning to lose heart in a big way. She couldn't escape, and she knew Ross wouldn't be there alone. The manipulating bastard never went anywhere without backup.

Her arm seared with pain, and her head throbbed. She felt weak and vulnerable, a feeling she had promised herself she had left behind when she escaped from Colin.

He was planning to ruin the rest of her life. She knew that. Even if Nathan managed to rescue her— which looked increasingly doubtful—he wouldn't want her once Colin had told him about her past. No matter what happened, her future with him was over. Within the next hour Colin would have robbed her of everything.

Mickey had his foot to the floor as they sped through the country roads, and Summer strained her eyes in the dark to find some way of identifying their whereabouts.

"You getting excited?" Colin jeered.

Summer stared at him, wondering, not for the first time, what she ever found attractive about the scumbag.

"You want us one at a time or all together?" Mickey's voice was as rough as gravel as he leered at her.

"I don't think there'll be time for taking turns," Colin laughed.

Summer felt bile rise in her throat, and she swallowed hard. This had to be her worst nightmare about to come true, and there was nothing she could do about it...or was there?

With no idea where they were, and no concept of time, her mind raced for clues. Harrison had a cell phone, so she had hope. No one had waved any weapons around, and she hadn't noticed any guns. Unless they had rifles in the back of the wagon or something.

"I need the toilet," she said, fidgeting a little.

Colin laughed derisively. "Well, that might make things a little easier for you then."

Mickey guffawed. He really was an ugly brute.

"Please, Colin. I won't try to get away or anything. Heck you can come with me if you want. I just really need to pee, that's all."

"Well, I ain't into them golden showers, so I suppose I might let you go, for a price." Colin leered at her, rubbing his hands on her breasts.

Summer immediately felt her stomach churn, and this time she couldn't control it. Colin finally got some comeuppance, courtesy of Nathan's delicious food.

"Stop this damn thing. I need to get out!" Colin cursed as Mickey drew to a halt on the back road.

Mickey jumped back into his door. Colin was already out, and Summer went to follow him.

"No you don't!" Mickey grabbed her by the arm and got caught in the crossfire of her upset stomach.

"You fucking cow!" Mickey opened his door and leaped out, yelling for Harrison.

Summer scooted over to the driver's seat and grabbed for the keys, still in the ignition.

"Forget it!" Harrison's big, hairy hand shot through the doorway and covered hers, squeezing her fingers tight.

Summer screamed. He hauled her out of the truck, and as he swung her around she grabbed the cell from his hip pocket and thrust it into her own, retching as she did so as to distract his attention.

"Don't you fucking dare barf over me, bitch!" Harrison growled, grabbing her good arm.

"I can't help it," she protested as unwelcome tears streamed down her face. She was standing squarely in front of him on the grass verge, while the other two removed their shirts and used them to wipe their bodies clean.

Knowing she didn't have much time she forced a gag and Harrison instinctively jumped backward, momentarily freeing her. She only needed that moment to run into the woodland at the side of the road.

"Get back here!" Harrison's voice rang in her ears as she clutched the cell from her pocket and ran as fast as she could into the trees. She could hear them coming after her, but none of them seemed to have torches or weapons.

She hid amid some bushes when she was far enough away. Her heart pounded painfully against her ribs, and she thought she was about to be sick again. She took the cell and dialed 911.

"Police. I'm in some woods by the road. About half an hour from Medley. Off the main road. There's three men coming. A white cottage was down the road, I think."

Her mind raced as she heard hefty footsteps coming

her way. She stuffed the cell back in her pocket without switching it off and crouched into a tight ball between the bushes.

She desperately wanted to get back to the road where she would have half a chance of a passing motorist seeing her, but she knew that these bastards would also see her.

"Which way?" Harrison's gruff voice could be heard through his wheezing.

"She can't have gone far. You better not tell Ross yet. He'll skin us alive for this." Colin panted as he barked his orders. He was good at that, at least.

"We haven't got long." Mickey caught up with them just a few feet from the bush where she was hiding.

Her heart was in her mouth, and she held her breath to try to keep quiet.

"Hello? Hello? Ma'am, are you there?" The operator's muffled voice rose from her pocket, and she grabbed the phone to silence the call.

Unfortunately her sudden movement caused a rustle of the nearby leaves.

"Did you hear something?" It was Mickey.

"Over there!" Colin's menacing snarl told her he was well and truly onto her, and she froze with fear.

Summer's eyes darted around for inspiration, and she found it in the form of a branch not far from where she hid.

"There!" Colin pointed to her just as she reached out, grabbed the wood, and sprang to her feet, tossing the cell deep into the bushes.

"Don't you come near me!" Her voice was shrill as she waved the branch to and fro in front of her.

The three men leaped back, gawping at her. Then Colin took a step closer, and she swung the branch, walloping him across his outstretched arm.

"Bitch!" He grabbed his injured arm and rubbed it, scowling at her.

"You just keep away and no one gets hurt!" she yelled.

"The hell we will. Get her!" Colin sneered as he waved his good arm at the other two, and suddenly she felt strong hands grab her from behind while someone yanked the branch from her grasp.

"Get your filthy hands off me, motherfucker!" she screamed as Harrison held her tight then lifted her off the ground and brutally carried her back toward the truck.

"You'll fucking pay for this, slut!" Colin promised her.

"Don't you dare threaten me." Summer didn't know whether she was more angry or scared, but she yelled at him anyhow.

Colin jumped in next to her while Mickey got back in the driver's seat and gunned the engine. This time Colin clamped her with his unforgiving grip as they set off back down the road, the men complaining about the stench of sick in the cab.

"He should be there by now," Harrison moaned from the back of the truck. "Hey, where the fuck's my phone?"

"She must have swiped it!" Colin held both her wrists in one of his hands while he checked her pockets. "What the hell have you done with it, slut?"

She shrugged. "Guess I dropped it."

"Fucking hell! Do you have any idea what you've just done? Ross'll be trying to contact us. He'll be livid when he arrives and we're not there." Harrison hollered through the window.

"You're dead. You do realize that, tramp?" Colin's smarmy voice was like a coating of black oil, suffocatingly thick and cloaked in darkness.

Summer swallowed hard. She hoped she had stalled them long enough not to give them time for any of their "fun" if nothing else. She still had a little while before they reached Ross. Maybe it would be enough? She had to hope. This bastard had taken almost everything but not her will to live.

Colin gripped her tightly by both wrists now.

"You're the one who'll be dead when the cops catch up with you!" she snapped.

Colin sneered. "You honestly think they'll find you out here? Forget it. It's so not happening."

An uneasy silence settled around them for the rest of the trip.

"We're here." Mickey shouted triumphantly about ten minutes later as he pulled off the track and parked behind a large black SUV.

"What the fuck time do you call this?" Ross's voice was as coarse as sandpaper as he hollered at the men.

He was a tall guy and wore a dark suit. His pitted skin meant he wasn't particularly good-looking, and he had short, sandy-colored hair and pale, mean eyes. He gave the impression of a smart businessman, but Summer knew the only business he was in was that of ruining lives.

Colin got out and yanked her from the cab of the truck.

"*Fuck*! What the hell's that stink?" Ross jerked back as they stood before him. Mickey and Harrison joined them.

"Fucking bitch barfed all over us," Mickey grumbled.

"Must have been excited at seeing you again, boss," Colin jeered.

Ross's look of disgust vanished as he guffawed. "Well, is that a fact? And have you got what I want, whore?"

"Oh, she's got it all right. Just not in money!" Colin snarled.

"No fucking money? What in hell do you think you're doing, bitch? We've been counting on you to bring home the fucking bacon!"

"Think you'll have to take it some other way," Harrison sneered, leering at Summer.

"I guess I know a few people who might pay me for her time, but I'll have to test her out myself first." Ross's laugh was evil, and Summer's stomach churned again.

He put out his hand to her, and Colin briefly let her go. She instinctively went to run, but Ross grabbed her by her bad arm. She shrieked with agony as he hauled her like a sack of potatoes toward his car.

"Get off me, you bastard!" she howled at him while tears flooded her face.

A siren wailed from the main road, and her heart leaped. The car in front of the squad car was the one that really gave her hope. It was silver and glinted in the dim light of the moon.

Nathan jumped out of the driver's side, a gun in his hand. "Drop your damn weapons," he yelled, inching toward them. Dominic was by his side, his gun aimed at the fuckers by the truck.

"What the...?" Ross immediately went to pull his gun from the holster under his arm. Summer felt him reach for it and knocked it clean out of his hand as he went to draw.

"*Fuck*!" the bastard cursed as it flew into the grass. He held her in front of him as he stretched to get it.

A shot was fired, and he slumped down to the ground, howling in agony. Blood poured from his hand where Nathan had shot him.

Adrenaline flooded Summer's veins, and she took one step closer and grabbed the gun before he had a chance to try again. She pointed it at Ross who lay on the ground staring up at her in disbelief.

"What the fuck?" Colin hollered, and she turned and pointed the gun at him instead. His glazed eyes were staring at her through the darkness, and she could see that his jaw had almost hit the ground. His hands were already behind his head, as Dominic had them all pinned helplessly against the truck.

Suddenly she now had a power over Colin that she'd only ever dreamed of. His life was in her hands—in her one finger. All the filthy, humiliating crap he'd put her through flashed in front of her eyes, like life to a dying man. Every time he had hurt her, frightened her, abused her. It was all there. It was all at the mercy of her finger. That man—that animal—would be gone forever. The relief swept through her at the very thought, and she narrowed her eyes, savoring the sensation. Her finger teased the trigger, her adrenaline running high.

"It's all right, sugar." A soft voice was in her ear, and a warm hand smothered hers. "Not like this."

As if in a daze, she looked up into Nathan's big, brown eyes. She was aware of him murmuring to her, and she slowly let him take the gun from her hand and give it to a nearby police officer. Then his warm arms enveloped her, and she sighed as his scent and his body wrapped her in a cloak of safety.

"You do know she's a whore, don't you?" Colin's gravelly voice scraped through her hazy thoughts.

"Shut it, scumbag!"

Summer quickly turned her head in shock. She had never heard Dominic use foul language before, although he had accused someone of talking bullshit in the MD's office that time.

A cop was cuffing Colin as he tried to taunt them, and Dominic thumped him in the mouth. Colin howled.

Summer looked back up at Nathan, who was smiling. She was vaguely aware of the cops removing Ross from the ground nearby as a police van arrived to cart them all away.

"They traced you by the cell phone," Nathan murmured in her ear. "They were already partway here after your bank card was used at the ATM."

Summer smiled. She felt as though everything was going on around her in slow motion, and she had a hard job understanding what was happening, but the important thing was that Nathan was here and she was safe.

"Miss Marsden, do you think you could show us where the cell phone is now? We think it might hold some interesting information," a cop was asking her.

She turned around to face him and had to grab Nathan as her head spun. "Umm, yeah," she mumbled.

Nathan was holding her tight, and she took a second to steady herself. Her head swam, and she still felt a little sick. Sick? *Damn!* She suddenly remembered that she had vomited on herself as well as those bastards, and here she was hugging Nathan! She tried to pull away from him, but he held her firmly.

"It's all right," he assured her calmly.

"But, I was sick. I stink!" she whispered.

Nathan chuckled and held her even tighter. "It doesn't matter. You're safe. That's all that matters." Summer felt her heart melt, and her body sank into him.

"I'll come with you," Nathan told the police officer and tossed his keys over to Dominic.

She was curled up safely in Nathan's arms as the policeman drove back down the road. She could just make out the area where the truck had pulled over for the men to get cleaned up.

"It's through there," she pointed as they parked.

"Can you show us exactly where, baby?" Nathan kissed her head.

"Yeah. I know where it was. There's a small clump of bushes. I was hiding there and..."

"Shh, it's all right."

Nathan had obviously noticed the tears that ran down her cheeks at the memory.

Summer cleared her throat and climbed out of the car. She led them over to where she had thrown the cell. A shiver ran down her spine as she recalled the terror she had felt while crouched here just a short while earlier.

"I threw it as hard as I could into the middle, so they wouldn't find it," she explained.

One of the officers retrieved the phone, still switched on. "I'm sure this will hold enough evidence not only to convict them but a few more of the gang as well. This will give us what we need to detain them all for quite a while." The officer grinned as he held the car door open for her to climb in.

"We'll stop by the emergency room and get you checked out before you go home," he told her as she snuggled into Nathan's side with a yawn.

Chapter Nine

Nathan waited anxiously for Summer to wake up. They had taken her to trauma to remove all the glass still left in her arm. The poor girl must have been in agony. She had a thick bandage on her forearm.

He'd managed to doze for a while, but the hospital chair wasn't very comfy and he longed to be back in his own bed, but only with Summer.

"Hey, sleepyhead. How're you feeling?" He smiled as he watched those massive green eyes slowly open, and she stared around the room.

"OK, I think." Her voice was small, and she looked bewildered.

"You're at the hospital. Some glass was still stuck in your arm, and they had to put you under to get it out. They'll check on you in a while and let you come home if you're up to it."

He leaned over and kissed her lightly on the cheek, noticing how her face fell at the mention of going home. He guessed what she was worried about.

"Dominic's arranging to have all your stuff brought over to my place. You'll stay with me for a while. You can decide what to do about your place later, but I'm not having you living there while it's not secure."

He studied her face for a reaction, knowing this could go one of two ways. She'd either be grateful or pissed.

She smiled, and he sighed with relief.

"OK, Sir," she said with a cheeky grin.

She was learning.

The doctor came in just then, so Nathan left the room while he checked her over.

"She might need this." The nurse came over and handed him a leaflet while he waited in the corridor.

It was information about counseling. Nathan thanked her, feeling a little uneasy. She'd been through a heck of a lot and having a professional to talk to might help, but he knew Summer would be reluctant. Hell, she hadn't told him or Dominic about her past, and he still had to find out what that asshole was inferring when he shouted all that shit about her being a whore. There was no way that was true.

And was that what he was referring to in that note when he threatened to tell her boss about her?

"Mr. Faulkner? You can take her home now. The

nurse will give you some painkillers for her, but other than that she just needs to take things easy for a while."

Nathan felt himself relax as he opened the door. Summer was sitting up in the bed with a worried expression. She wore a hospital gown, and he guessed right away what she was thinking. He took off his shirt and handed it to her.

"You'd best wear this for a while." He couldn't help grinning as he watched her take in his naked chest. He felt a warm glow inside and automatically cocked an eyebrow at her, questioningly. "Your clothes are covered in vomit."

Poor Summer looked mortified. Her big eyes darted away from him, and a deep chuckle escaped his throat.

"Um, I'm sorry," she mumbled, taking the shirt from him.

"Hey, I believe it's what got you out of this mess."

She nodded, still diverting her eyes from his face.

"Want some help getting changed?"

She shook her head. "I can manage."

Nathan couldn't help noticing that she looked sad. She was probably recalling all that shit.

"Mr. Faulkner, here's the meds she needs and her things." A nurse handed him a couple of bags.

"Here, let me help you, dear." She immediately went over to Summer and helped her out of her gown.

Damn, he'd wanted to do that. Nathan decided to do the gentlemanly thing and wait out in the corridor.

"Everything OK?" Dominic arrived while he was staring out the window.

"Hey, buddy. Yeah, I'm taking her home now."

"Great. I've brought your car. Heaven's on her way over with mine." Dominic looked cheerful and very casual in his jeans and T-shirt. He tossed him the keys.

"Heaven?" Nathan smirked.

"Yeah. I thought it would be good to get help from a woman when I went to pack up Summer's stuff. Heaven was glad to help."

"Yeah, I'll bet." Nathan grinned, admiring his friend's ability to keep his expressionless demeanor.

Dominic's cell beeped, and he went to answer it. "Heaven's here. She's bringing some clothes for Summer."

"That's real thoughtful," Nathan managed.

He'd kinda liked the idea of her wearing his shirt.

"Hey guys." Heaven smiled as she rushed over to them. "How is she?"

Nathan grinned, noticing her eyes go a little wider when she saw he wasn't wearing a shirt.

"Good timing. She's going home." Dominic smiled at her. Huh, that was strange. When this was all settled down, he'd have to rib his buddy a little about that.

"Shall I take these in?" Heaven had a bright smile as she held up a bag.

Nathan nodded, a little reluctantly. He had been looking forward to seeing Summer in nothing but a shirt —*his* shirt.

He could hear excited chatter as Heaven entered the little side room and smiled to himself. Heaven would be a good friend for Summer. The redhead was a little older than her and was a real good sub. Summer could learn a lot from her.

His mind wandered a little at the thought of Summer's submissive nature; she had been wonderful in the bedroom, but keeping secrets and getting caught up in all this bullshit was certainly not submissive behavior. He'd have to have words with her about that.

"Time for a coffee?" Dominic smiled.

"Yeah, we may as well. Once the women start gassing we could be here all day."

"Don't you think you'd better get dressed first?" Dominic smirked.

Nathan chuckled. "Summer was going to wear it home," he explained, holding up the bag of dirty clothes.

Dominic nodded. "The car's just outside. I'll go put these in the trunk while you go in."

"Cheers, buddy." Nathan handed back the keys and the two bags.

He knocked on the side room door before going in. He could hear them chattering away from outside.

"Hey, I thought you might have finished with my shirt." He was pleased to see that Summer looked a little sad to return it to him.

"Thanks anyway," she said with a small smile.

"We're just going to grab a coffee while you finish up," he told them.

"We won't be long. They can follow you down," the nurse said.

Nathan noticed that she had another of those counseling leaflets in her hand and retreated gratefully.

"I've got some news," Dominic confided as they sat in the hospital cafeteria drinking coffee. It was midmorning and the place was jumping. "That club Summer was working at was a strip joint."

Nathan stared at him as a cold lump sank in his stomach. "What in hell was she doing there?" He hardly dared ask.

Dominic shook his head. "It's all very hush-hush. No one will tell me."

Nathan sighed. "Well, I'll have to ask her then." He took another sip of his coffee.

"I presume that must have been what the asshole was trying to threaten her about. He hoped she'd lose her job once we found out." Dominic sat back casually in his chair, frowning at a dirty mark on his cup.

"Heh! He doesn't know us, does he?" Nathan smirked.

Dominic grinned. "If the sight of a naked woman was going to shock us we'd have no dang staff."

Nathan chuckled, recalling the sight of Summer naked. She was absolutely gorgeous.

"Hey, they're here." Dominic drank the rest of his coffee as he stood up.

"All ready," Heaven announced with a smile.

Summer looked a little nervous and very fragile. She had obviously just taken a shower, as she looked refreshed and her hair was still damp.

Nathan stood up and put an arm around her. He felt her warm body snuggle into his and grinned.

"Time to get you home, sugar."

She looked up at him and nodded gratefully.

"Well, thanks for all your help, you two. I really appreciate it." Nathan shook Dominic's hand and gave Heaven a small peck on the cheek as they went their separate ways.

The journey home was quiet, and Nathan noticed Summer's big, sad eyes gazing out of the window.

"You OK, sugar?"

She turned back to him, and he noticed her eyes looked watery. "I'm fine," she told him with a weak smile that didn't reach her eyes.

"Tired?"

"A little."

"Too tired to talk?"

The atmosphere in the car suddenly turned to ice. Summer's eyes shot back to the road, and her muscles tensed instantly.

"The cops're coming over later to speak to you," he told her slowly.

"I'm not a whore," she blurted out as tears streamed down her pale cheeks.

"I know that, sugar." Nathan placed a hand on hers and felt her shivering. She was dressed in jeans and a shirt, and it was quite a warm day, but the poor girl was like an iceberg.

She looked up at him gratefully, her eyes wide.

"Really? You didn't believe him?"

Nathan shook his head. "He's an asshole."

He watched her snigger and noticed the relief sweep across her face as her body began to relax. He pulled up on the drive and quickly went around to help her out of the car. He grabbed her stuff from the trunk and took her inside.

He went to make lunch as Summer went straight to the utility to wash her clothes. The poor thing seemed so embarrassed about being sick. Nathan reckoned she must have been terrified to throw up like that.

She came back into the kitchen as he placed some ham-filled baguettes and salad on the table.

"Heaven and Dominic even got the food in," Nathan said as they sat down.

"They've brought everything over from my apartment," Summer said in a small voice.

Nathan felt his stomach churn. "Are you OK with that? We thought you wouldn't want to go back there after what happened, and it's not secure anyhow."

He took a bite of his bread as he studied her. He could almost see the cogs turning in her head as she considered what he said.

"That's real kind." She smiled and helped herself to salad.

"Summer, if you want to go back there you can, but

I'd like to get a few security measures in place first. The doc reckons you need looking after for a few days, so I thought it best to bring you back here, for a while at least. You can take your time and consider what to do next." He placed a hand on hers and felt her relax a little more.

"It's real nice of you to let me stay here, but I still need to get to work. Will I be able to get a bus from here?" She frowned, and he could see that she was working everything through in her head.

"You won't be working for a few days, sugar. You need to rest. After that we'll figure something out." He felt his jaw clench as he watched her expression, half expecting her to object. She didn't disappoint.

"I'm fine, really. I don't have another shift until tomorrow anyway, and I'll have had a good rest by then. I need this job, Nathan. I'm relying on the income."

"Why do you need it so badly?" He took another drink of his coffee, studying her face.

She sighed, as if weighing up whether or not to tell him. "I have debts to pay."

"Your debts or Cromer's?"

"That's debatable, but actually they're in my name so legally they're mine. I've tried arguing about it, but it's no good." She bit her lip. "If I can just get a few more shifts at the restaurant it'll enable me to cover my current rent and bills as well as make inroads into the other stuff. It's accruing interest, so I've got to get it paid off as soon as possible."

He could see that she had it all sorted out in her head and wouldn't welcome any interference, but he was going to have to try.

"What sort of debts are they? Bank? Credit cards? Loans?"

He stared at her face as a myriad of emotions passed over it. She clearly didn't want to tell him.

"There's various ones. I'm hoping I won't have to pay Ross now that the police have got him, although it's possible he'll have friends who might come looking for the payment."

"You bought drugs off the guy?" Nathan had a sick feeling in his gut. He knew she was no junkie, but Alex Ross was a well-known dealer even in these parts.

She shook her head. "No, Colin Cromer bought the drugs. He started off working for the guy and then ended up using the stuff himself. When he couldn't pay up he told Ross that I'd pay."

Nathan felt a wrench in his stomach. "Why would you do that?"

"Because I wanted to live. Colin was a real violent bastard. I couldn't exactly refuse. That's why I worked four jobs at once, just trying to keep him happy while I figured out a way to escape."

She took another drink of her coffee, and Nathan could see that she was fighting back tears.

"And one of those jobs was in a strip joint?" He

watched as sadness cloaked her face, and she blushed slightly.

"Yes. I was a pole dancer. I didn't do lap dances or private shows or have sex with the clients; I just danced on a podium. I needed the money." She sighed.

Nathan squeezed her hand gently. "Why didn't you just leave him?"

"I did. It made things ten times worse. He's got contacts everywhere—or Ross has. When he caught up with me he beat me black and blue. He told me I owed him."

"How in hell did he work that one out?" Nathan felt his blood begin to boil as he stared incredulously at her flushed, sad expression.

Just then the doorbell rang and Summer jumped, panic spreading across her face. Nathan rubbed her hand with his. "That'll be the cops. Finish your lunch."

He was pleased to see Steve Ratner standing on his doorstep, along with one of his colleagues.

"Come on in. We're just finishing up lunch," Nathan told them with a smile. "She's a little fragile, so go easy, buddy." He murmured into Steve's ear, and the big cop nodded with a smile.

"We won't take long. Those bastards were singing like blue jays down at the station. It's amazing what they'll do when they're desperate for their next fix." Steve shook his head as they went into the kitchen.

Nathan made the introductions and offered the cops some coffee while they all sat around the table.

"Summer's worried that Ross is going to send his heavies around to collect payment for Cromer's debts," Nathan announced as he piled up the plates.

Steve shook his head, smiling. "You've got nothing to worry about there, darlin'," he assured her. "We had a good look through the contacts on that phone you gave us. I'd be surprised if there's any of Ross's gang not in a cell as we speak. Oh, and talking of Cromer's debts, here's the ten dollars he took from your bank account."

Summer sighed and smiled gratefully at the cop. "Thank you."

"Hey, we've been after that load of scum for a while now. Thought they'd made their way up the coast. You managed to hand them to us on a plate, so it's us who need to be thanking you." Steve gave her a shit-eating grin and a wink.

"So, am I safe now?" Summer's voice was small and weak, and Nathan couldn't resist placing his hand over hers again. She looked so vulnerable and scared, it made his gut twist.

"You're with me now, sugar. Of course you're safe." He watched her give him a shy smile and felt a glow inside his stomach.

Steve nodded. "You need to listen to him, darlin'. They're out of the way now. You can get on and enjoy your life without looking over your shoulder."

She nodded.

"There's just one or two questions the officer needs

to ask you about Cromer, if that's all right?" Steve asked with a reassuring smile.

"Of course." Summer managed a weak smile back while Nathan and Steve left them at the table.

"What do you think?" Nathan murmured once they were at the far end of the large kitchen.

"That bastard's given her a hell of a ride. Threatened her with all sorts of shit. No wonder she was scared sick of him," Steve confided.

Nathan gritted his teeth. "Just give me two minutes alone with him, buddy."

Steve smirked, and Nathan knew he felt the same way. "Wish I could, bud. Heck, I'd give you a hand."

They both sniggered.

"Is she in any danger now?" Nathan murmured.

Steve sighed. "I don't think so, but best be vigilant for a while, just in case any more scum come crawling out of the woodwork. We've got the ringleaders, anyhow."

The police officer gestured to his boss, and he and Nathan went back to the table.

"Miss Marsden's concerned about how they came to find her. Apparently a female at the club was seeing one of Ross's associates and tipped them off."

Nathan felt his blood run cold. "A member of the staff?" He stared at Summer. She looked nervous.

"That's what Colin said."

"That's interesting. Have they hired any other new staff lately?" Steve asked Nathan.

Searching his brain, Nathan could come up with

nothing. He would know of any changes in staff because of the wages, but he couldn't recall anyone. He shook his head. "We always check out new staff thoroughly. We'd know if they had any unsavory connections."

Summer stared at him. "You check out who staff hang out with? Is that legal?" She looked horrified, and he couldn't help feeling a little sorry for her. She must have been feeling betrayed.

"We don't stalk them or anything. We just have inside information about who staff associate with. It's a security measure for the club. If one of the staff is seeing one of Ross's men they've either just started a new relationship or they've done a damn good job in hiding it." He frowned.

Nathan didn't like to think of any of the staff being dishonest, especially in this sort of matter.

"So how come you didn't know about me?" Summer's chin jutted out, and she appeared a little defiant and annoyed.

"It takes us a short while to get that sort of information together," Nathan explained. "We know who the local undesirables are and who they hang out with. We didn't expect Ross to be back in the area. He obviously wasn't until they followed you here.

"Dominic Ray's a shrewd judge of character though. He can usually tell straight away if someone's trouble or not. He had a good feeling about you. You wouldn't have got the job otherwise."

He was surprised to see a flash of anger in Summer's eyes, which she quickly averted.

"We'll get over to the club now," Steve said, tucking his notebook into his breast pocket. "HR should know if there's been any change in anyone's circumstances. I'll keep my ear to the ground."

Nathan saw them out while Summer tidied the kitchen.

"Are you OK, sugar?" Nathan wandered back into the room to find Summer staring out of the window.

She jumped when she heard him, and he cursed himself for frightening her. He walked over slowly and put his arms around her waist. "You look tired. Why don't you go take a nap?" he murmured into her ear as the smell of her honey shampoo wafted delicately into his face.

"I think the counselor's coming by today," she said quietly.

"OK. I'll be here," he assured her.

"You don't have to go to work today?" She frowned.

"I might drop by the office later. But I won't be leaving you on your own, so don't you worry about that."

Summer nodded and went to the bedroom.

Nathan felt his stomach churn. She was still in danger, and she obviously realized it, despite what Steve Ratner had said. He seethed. Hadn't she been through enough already?

Chapter Ten

The next few days passed really slowly for Summer. Nathan lavished lots of care on her and held her every night when they were in bed together. She was surprised how easy he was to talk to, and she felt relieved to explain about her past and her terrifying relationship with Colin Cromer.

She could tell Nathan was seething when she told him what it had been like, and he held her even tighter and assured her that it was all over now.

She had met a counselor, Becky Truman, who had been to visit her every day, and had told her how Colin had made her feel and the horrors she had been threatened with for not complying with his wishes. It helped, a little.

Nathan had even got a lawyer friend of his to come and take details about the credit card Colin had run up in her name. He was confident that she wasn't liable for the debt and had assured her that Colin Cromer would be facing up to his own responsibility. And facing charges for fraud at the same time.

"Heaven's here," Nathan told her as she sat in the garden, enjoying the late afternoon sun.

Summer smiled. Heaven had been to see her every day since she had come home and was great company. She was full of funny stories about the club and had Summer in stitches most of the time. It had enabled Nathan to go into work for a few hours, as he kept his promise of never leaving her alone.

"Hi, you're looking better," Heaven told her with a big smile.

"I am. I'll be going back to work, soon." Summer was feeling really buoyant today. "And guess what? Nathan's got me an interview with the finance director for the clerk's job. Apparently the guy's really flexible and is happy to see me as soon as I'm up to it." She beamed.

"That's great," Heaven said, smiling first at her and then at Nathan.

"Beats that crummy grocery store anyway," Nathan murmured. "By the way, where was that place, again?"

Summer giggled. She had told them both the story of her dreadful induction into the life of a shelf-stacker, and they'd had a good laugh about it.

"It was a Ms. Powell, and it was just near the bus stop in Clifford Street. It's filthy though. Don't buy anything from there whatever you do!"

Nathan snorted. "Don't worry about that, sugar. I don't intend to."

"Oh, but I heard the floor's really clean," Heaven piped up, and they all burst out laughing.

Nathan went to answer the phone while the girls chatted.

"Do you know when you'll be coming back to the restaurant? We could do with some excitement around the place," Heaven asked, slumping into the rattan chair next to Summer.

"Tomorrow, I hope. Nathan said I might be able to see about the finance job and just pop my head in to see you all. I'm not allowed to start back in the restaurant for a day or two though. Dominic doesn't want me working near the food so soon after being sick."

"Yeah, Dominic's a bit of a stickler for the rules," Heaven said, thoughtfully.

"You like him, don't you?" Summer narrowed her eyes while she studied her friend.

Heaven grinned. "Not in the way you mean. He's more like a brother to me than anything else. We've known each other for a quite a while."

Summer pouted. She had hoped for some romantic gossip about the two of them.

"But at least he's not married," Heaven pointed out, setting them both off into fits of giggles again.

"Good news." Nathan returned with a tray of cold drinks. "Master Steve said they've made eleven arrests so far, and they expect to make even more when they've followed up a few more leads."

Heaven beamed. "I knew he would. He's the best." She took a sip of her drink.

"That's great," Summer said with a relieved sigh.

"Still no news about who tipped them off at the club?" Heaven frowned.

Nathan shook his head. "Nope. HR has checked through their records, and there's been no change of address or anything for quite a while. I suppose Cromer could have been lying just to worry you."

Summer felt his eyes on her, and she shook her head. "No, that's not his style. He'd relish worrying me, but he's not clever enough to make up a story like that."

"Well, if you ladies want to gossip for an hour I wouldn't mind popping down to the club to check on things." Nathan kissed Summer on the top of her head, and she felt herself glow inside.

It was the little things that Nathan did and said that made the world of difference to her.

"Oh, I think we could manage that," Heaven told him with a smile.

"So how are things at the club?" Summer asked once they were alone.

"Busy. The sommelier's still off sick. Dominic thinks he's found another job and is trying it out for a while before resigning from the club. One of our regulars reckons they've seen him at a bar downtown. He's not sure if he was actually working there or not though." Heaven sounded conspiratorial, and Summer guessed it wasn't common knowledge.

"What's he going to do?"

"Check it out, I guess. Those Doms have contacts all over the place." Heaven grinned as she took another sip of her drink.

"Yeah. So I've heard. Nathan reckons they even find out who potential staff are friends with before they give them a job." She looked down at her hands.

"It's to protect all of us," Heaven assured her. "You know how it is with BDSM, you have to be safe. If they let people in who aren't who they claim to be, or have suspect friends, it could put the whole club in danger."

Summer felt a thud in her stomach, and she stared at her friend.

"Do they think that's what I've done? Have I brought trouble to the club because of my past? Is that why they won't let me come back?" She shot to her feet as the realization hit her.

"No, of course not." Heaven stood up quickly, a hand on Summer's arm. "You didn't bring trouble to anyone. You were a victim, that's all."

Summer stared into her face, studying it for any sign she was lying. There wasn't any. She still wasn't happy though. It was all starting to add up.

"I've got to go." Summer rushed to the bedroom and started stuffing her belongings into a bag.

"What are you doing? You're supposed to be staying here," Heaven protested, following her into the room.

"Why? To keep me out of the way? To save me being a nuisance to everyone? To stop me causing trouble?"

"No, of course not."

"I'm better now. I don't need Nathan to look after me. And if they don't want me at the club, that's fine. I'll find another job."

Summer threw her things together angrily, shrugging off Heaven's arms as she tried to stop her.

"I've had enough of conforming to what someone else wants. I'm not being pushed around anymore. I can look after myself, and I damn well intend to!"

"Summer, you're overreacting. You've got it all wrong."

"Good. In that case there's no problem, is there?" Her teeth were gritted as she stormed out of the house and hailed a cab.

Summer didn't even know where Nathan's house was, so there was no way she could have negotiated buses to get home. Besides that, her bag was heavy and she wasn't quite as strong as she had made out.

As she neared her apartment she felt a dull thud in the pit of her stomach. She was beginning to calm down a little and wondered if she had done the right thing in storming out like that. She really liked Nathan. Heck, she might even love him. She knew she would miss him.

But there was no way she could stay there, just being

kept out of the way. She wasn't a child, and she was damned if she was going to be treated like one. OK, so they might not want her to work at Collar and Cuffs because of her past, but that didn't mean she had to be a prisoner in Nathan's house.

Although, it was a beautiful house...

The cab cost her almost all of her cash, but at least she was home. She opened her door as memories flooded back of how she had left.

Slamming the door behind her, she was stunned to hear an odd beeping sound. She turned to the source of the noise and found a touchpad on the wall in the hall-way. She stared at it in disbelief. An intruder alarm had been installed. The beeping became more urgent, and her heart raced as she tried to decide what the code would be.

Not even knowing who had installed the contrap-tion, she had no idea what combination they might have used. She tried the obvious one: 1, 2, 3, 4, 5, 6. No luck. She tried 0, 9, 8, 7, 6, 5. Still no luck. She punched numbers in to make different patterns across the board, a square, a letter Z. The beeping was becoming manic now, and she panicked at the thought of the alarm going off. In desperation she punched in her date of birth. Relief! Whoever had had it put in obviously knew that much about her.

She slumped on the couch with a sigh. The house looked empty. All of her ornaments and photographs had gone. The walls were bare of all pictures. And she noticed the smell of paint.

Seething, she went into the bedroom. All the furniture had been moved to the middle of the room and dust covers had been used to cover it and the carpet.

Cans of paint had been placed in one corner, ready for use, and a small patch of pale pink had been painted onto the wall under the window.

In a fury she checked out the rest of the apartment. Every wall had been stripped and most of the curtains had been removed.

Someone had decided to redecorate her home. If it wasn't for the fact that her furniture and a few of her knickknacks were still there, she would have worried that she had been evicted. She'd only been gone a few days!

She went back to the lounge and slumped angrily onto the sofa. How dare they? How dare anyone take over her home like this?

Hot tears poured down her cheeks at the audacity of it all. She had got this place looking as nice as she could, and she was proud of it. How dare someone come in and decide to change it all?

A knock at the door made her jump, and she wiped her face angrily. She strode over to open it and gaped as she noticed all the bolts and heavy-duty locks that had been attached to her front door.

Clenching her teeth in anger she swung it open to see Nathan standing there. She glared at him.

"May I come in?" He looked angry. How dare he look angry?

"No." She flung the door to close it, but his foot barred the way.

"Don't be childish, Summer. I need to talk to you." His voice was clipped, which irked her even more.

"Well, you didn't need to talk to me before wrecking my home. Or was that nothing to do with you?" She spat the words at him accusingly.

He sighed and strode across the threshold. "You need to put the chain on before you open the door," he told her, sliding it across the door as he closed it.

"I don't use chains on my door. Neither do I use intruder alarms," she told him coldly.

"You do now."

She shot him a black look and was astonished to receive an even darker one in return. She folded her arms defiantly.

"Heaven rang me. She was upset."

Summer felt herself go hot. She hadn't meant to upset her friend but was damned if she was going to be berated for it by Nathan.

"I'm upset too. I've come back to my home to find that someone's taken it over and done all this." She waved her arm at the room. "The last time I was here I was hurt and kidnapped. Now I've come back to find this mess. Do you know who would do such a cruel thing?" Her teeth were clenched as she glared at him.

Nathan sighed and sat on the sofa. "It was going to be a surprise for you if you decided to come back to live here. Otherwise at least it would be a nice, secure home for someone else to live in."

"If I decided to come back to live here? As opposed

to what? Letting the fuckers scare me out of my own home? Do you really think I'm that pathetic? You really don't know me at all, do you?" she screamed at him as anger boiled in her veins.

"As opposed to living with me. I was hoping you might have wanted to stay with me, that's all. I can see I was wrong. I obviously misunderstood what we had between us. I'm sorry. I'll get someone around first thing tomorrow to put everything back as it was." He spoke quietly as he got up and went to leave.

Summer felt a wrench in her gut. He was so handsome and had tried to do something to help her, but she was too angry to appreciate it. She just felt furious that he was now making her feel guilty because of it.

"Good. I want that damn alarm taken out too and my door returned to normal, without any holes." She spat the words, just as angry with herself as she was with him.

She couldn't bear to look at his face as he left. She just heard the door slam and collapsed on the sofa in a heap of tears. His words rang in her ears as she sobbed herself to sleep. *I obviously misunderstood what we had between us.*

It was pitch black when she awoke with a crick in her neck from her awkward position on the small sofa.

She felt cold and miserable. She was also alone and vulnerable. She shivered as she went straight over to the front door and locked it, using every bolt. She sighed, feeling a modicum of safety.

Pulling the dust cover off her bed, she noticed it had a change of bedding on it. The bloodstained coverlet was gone and in its place was her spare bedspread. Someone had been thoughtful enough to change it for her. She felt an ache in her heart.

With everything moved to the center of the room, it didn't look like her bedroom at all. She was grateful for it. Lying on her bed in the semi-darkness, she wasn't haunted with the visions of that dreadful attack.

The smell of paint made it seem like a new room, even though very little of it had made it onto the walls yet. Without curtains at the windows the moon was allowed to shine in, affording a dim glow to the whole room.

She watched the moon winking at her and wondered whether Nathan was watching it too. His words were still churning around and around inside her head, and she wondered what he had meant. Did he really think there was something between them? Did he really want her to move in with him?

He must have cared about her to get her apartment secured and redecorated for her. She recalled that he'd mentioned making it safe, but she hadn't expected this. What was she to do now?

Should she go back and ask him to take her back? Should she stay here and decorate the place herself? Did she really want to carry on living here? Alone?

She felt a cold chill run down her back. She wished she was in Nathan's bed, snuggling up to his warmth, his scent, his safety. She could relax when she was with him. He seemed to take her worries away from her. She felt tears trickle down her face again as her heavy eyes gradually closed.

Summer was awakened the next morning by the sound of a telephone ringing. Jumping from the bed, she bemoaned the fact that she hadn't even bothered to get undressed last night and was now uncomfortable and ill-rested. She was also shocked because she didn't own a phone.

She looked all around and saw a sleek cell sitting on her nightstand.

"Hello?"

"Hi Miss Marsden. My name's Cerys Simpson, and I'm calling from the finance office at Collar and Cuffs." The lady on the other end sounded very friendly and cheerful. Summer felt a lurch in her stomach, suddenly recalling the job she was hoping to get there.

"Oh, good morning."

"I understand that you might be interested in the vacancy for a part-time finance clerk here and am calling to ask if you would be free to come for an interview today."

Summer had a sudden feeling of dread. She wasn't

sure whether Nathan and Dominic would approve of her still going for the position, after all. It did look very much as though they didn't want her at the club. However, she needed a job. And this job would be suitably well paid.

"Miss Marsden?"

"Um...oh yes. Yes please. What time should I come?" she stammered.

"Can you make it at eleven thirty?"

Excitement welled inside her. "Yes, of course."

"Great. Just come to reception and ask for Cerys Simpson. I'll see you then."

"Thank you. Thank you so much."

Summer bit her lip as she clicked the phone off and replaced it on the stand.

She hummed as she dived into the shower and relished the hot water. She pulled out her gray shift dress, which she teamed with red pumps and a matching clutch.

Her makeup was immaculate, and even her hair behaved itself today. She felt like a million dollars as she raced out of the house to catch the bus. She was surprised to find that she was actually early, and, rather than wait in line, she popped into a small café and ordered a coffee.

Checking her change she realized that she even had enough left for a couple of rounds of toast, which she enjoyed before setting off back to the bus stop.

She arrived at Collar and Cuffs with ten minutes to spare, so she went straight to the powder room before reporting to reception. She was touching up her lipstick when a familiar face entered the room.

"Hi Mandy." She smiled, remembering the girl who helped her with her uniform and locker when she had first started there.

Mandy gaped at her. "Wh-what are you doing here?" She looked as though she had just seen a ghost.

"I've got an interview for the finance clerk's job," Summer told her with a grin.

Another girl came in just afterward. Summer thought she recognized her as the girl who was on the reception desk on her first day at the club. The girl looked surprised to see her, but Summer just smiled.

"Wish me luck," she said as she made her way to the door.

"Um...yeah." Mandy still looked shocked, and Summer wondered if it was because she looked so different from the last time they had met. She was really pleased with her look, and she straightened her hem as she went back out into the foyer.

Taking a deep breath, she was about to approach the front desk when she realized she had left her lipstick on the vanity. She quickly turned and went back into the ladies' room.

A voice came from one of the stalls. "I thought you said she'd left."

"Something must have gone wrong. She's not supposed to be here. They were going to scare her off at least. Ross wants her dead. I'll have to ask Darren what the hell's going on." Mandy's voice came from the other stall, and Summer's blood ran cold.

She quickly retrieved her lipstick, just as she heard the flush from one of the stalls, and rushed out into reception.

Chapter Eleven

"Miss Marsden? I'm Cerys. Do come through." A really elegant-looking lady with a stern black bob and a navy suit came to meet her at the front desk.

Summer's mind was reeling. "Yes, hi." She shook the lady's hand and was pleased to receive a warm smile.

"Come with me. I'll show you the department before you see the director."

Summer was relieved. She felt so tense she wasn't sure she could face some hoity-toity finance director right at this minute. Cerys seemed really friendly though, and she began to relax a little as they chatted.

The department wasn't as big as he expected. It seemed that Cerys did almost everything herself there and was glad of an extra pair of hands.

The section itself comprised a largish room with

several locked filing cabinets and numerous shelves with files on them, all plain black with neat white labels. A small desk sat by the window, which Cerys informed her would be hers, should she take the job.

There would be plenty of filing to do, and she was to take all the calls before putting them through to Cerys or the FD.

Cerys had a little office just off the main one and a small corridor lead down to the FD's.

"Let's have some coffee," Cerys offered after showing her where everything was kept. She led her into her office, which was small but immaculate.

Summer took the opportunity to study her would-be boss a little closer.

Cerys must have been in her late twenties or early thirties and was nothing short of beautiful. Her hair was sleek and perfect, and her makeup was flawless. Her bright red lipstick made her smile shine, and her big dark eyes twinkled, hinting at a sense of humor under her austere appearance. She was enviably slender, and her legs looked long and lithe in her heels, which must have been at least four inches high.

"Have you worked in finance before?" Cerys asked as they sipped their coffee.

"No. But I've worked in stores and offices."

"That should help you," Cerys said with a smile. "Are you used to answering the phone and fielding calls? The FD can be hard to get hold of at times, so you might need to take messages or put his calls through to me."

Summer felt a jolt in her stomach. The FD sounded like a bit of a tyrant, and she wasn't looking forward to meeting him. "I can do that." She tried to sound confident.

"The FD can also be a little awkward at times. Are you used to dealing with people like that?"

"Yes, all the time." Summer giggled.

"Good. You need the patience of a saint sometimes, but what can I say? He's a man, after all." Cerys winked at her and they both laughed.

"What sort of hours would I be working?" Summer asked as she sipped her coffee.

"We'll work out the specifics later, but it will be during the day. We don't open the office at night. I understand that you'll be working in the restaurant too, so we'll have to accommodate that. It's three nights a week at the moment, isn't it?" Cerys consulted a sheet of paper written in shorthand, so Summer wasn't able to understand it.

"That's right. I only started last week, and Dominic... er...Mr. Ray said he would let me know which nights would be my regular ones."

"Dominic's very pleased with your work," Cerys said with a smile, putting the paper back on her desk. "He thinks you'll fit in well here."

Summer felt herself blush. It was evident that they had been talking about her already, and she found Dominic so difficult to read that she hadn't been sure what he thought of her.

"I hope so. I like it here." She smiled and finished her coffee. She thought about how Dominic must really want her to stay working here, or else he wouldn't have put in such a good word for her. Her stomach lurched a little at the thought that she might have got things totally wrong last night, and now she'd upset Heaven and lost Nathan.

"Is everything all right?" Cerys looked concerned, and Summer realized she must have been frowning.

She smiled. "Yes, of course. I just wasn't aware that Dominic liked me, that's all. It's hard to tell, sometimes."

Cerys smiled back, putting down her cup. "Don't ever try to second-guess the men around here, Summer. They're a different breed. You can never tell what they're thinking, so it's best not to even try."

"I guess you're right." Summer sighed, thinking about Dominic and Nathan.

She really thought Dominic was going to fire her the other day, and she was still reeling about what Nathan had said last night about them having something between them. He didn't speak about his feelings much, although he was very demonstrative physically.

She couldn't help smiling when she realized that he thought they had something going between them, because she hadn't been sure if she was just imagining it all.

"Are you ready to meet the FD?" Cerys got up, straightening her skirt.

Summer felt a lurch in her stomach. She might have

impressed Cerys, but if the FD didn't like her she had no chance of getting this job.

"Wait in here. He'll be back in just a minute," Cerys said, showing her into the finance director's office.

"Thank you."

Summer's feet sank into the soft pile of the plush, cream carpet, and she gaped at the huge room. Filing cabinets lined one wall, with shelves full of the matching folders from the main office. A huge desk dominated the room, with a massive picture window behind it, showing a magnificent view of the surroundings from their position on the upper floor.

The whole room was bright and airy, and the clean lines and immaculate tidiness gave it a feeling of strict organization.

Summer stood staring out of the window. It was lunchtime, and people in suits lined the streets in the distance. Around the club there was a steady stream of people coming in for the restaurant, neatly dressed and unhurried.

"Don't turn around." A deep voice came from behind her, and she felt herself boil inside. She knew that voice. It was the voice of her Dom. The voice he used when they were in the dungeon together. The voice that made her cream in the sheer anticipation of what he had in mind.

She straightened her back and continued to stare out of the window, although she wasn't seeing the city now.

"For someone who wants a job in finance you're not very good at adding up, are you, Miss Marsden?"

Summer felt herself glow even hotter, and she thought she was about to spontaneously combust. Her mouth was suddenly dry, and she couldn't speak.

"You got it all wrong, sugar." His voice was a little gentler now, and she longed for him to touch her. She was also desperate to see his handsome face, to stare into his big, brown eyes. But she daren't. It wasn't that she was afraid to turn around, she just felt... compliant.

She closed her eyes while he spoke.

"You weren't being kept at my house to keep you out of the way. It was to keep you safe. I wanted to look after you, to make sure you were OK. I was having your place made safe because I know what an independent woman you are and that there was every chance you might want to go back there. I don't want you to live there, I want you to live with me.

"However, I want you to be happy, and if you think we're moving a little fast I understand that. If you must live at that apartment I would feel a lot better knowing that you were safe there. That's why I got security installed. The painters were just going to give the place a fresh lick of paint to make it feel a little more comfortable for you. I don't know, maybe dispel a few ghosts that might be lurking there after what happened."

Tears began to trail down Summer's face as he explained his motives, and she felt like a prize bitch for not realizing that in the first place. She had been far too angry and indignant to think straight last night, but now it all made sense. God, she was so stupid!

His voice deepened again. "Now, about this job. I need someone who can think logically—not go off half-cocked. Do you think you could manage that?"

"Yes, Sir." She breathed the words, which fell easily from her mouth.

"And I need someone who will listen to me, not hear half a story and make up the rest. Can you do that?"

His sultry tone made her clench her thighs as she felt herself get wetter. "Yes, Sir."

"And above all I need someone who is honest. Integrity is everything in the world of finance, and the staff who work here must be completely up front and truthful. Veracity is essential in all things, do you understand?"

"Yes, Sir." She knew he wasn't just talking about the job.

His tone became less stern and more sensual. "Now, how much do you want to work for me?"

Summer squeezed her thighs together as she heard his murmur right behind her now. He was so close she could smell that gorgeous scent he always wore.

"I-I want to," she whispered, her throat dry.

"Are you sure?"

"Yes. One hundred percent."

He chuckled. It was deep in his throat and made her feel even hotter all over.

"Think you're up to the job?"

"God, yes," she whispered again, unable to manage anything more.

Her heart hammered against her ribs just knowing he was right next to her. She squeezed her eyes tight shut to stop herself from looking at him. Although right at that moment she was unable to move anyway.

His hands caressed her upper arms, and she almost felt a sizzle. He nuzzled her hair, and she felt herself getting wetter and hotter.

"I missed you last night," he whispered softly. A massive lump formed in her throat, and she felt another tear trickle down her boiling face.

"I missed you too," she admitted in a barely audible whisper.

He ran a hand gently through her hair and kissed her neck lovingly, and she felt herself melt into his strong embrace. He stroked her arms up and down slowly, and she felt like she was about to burst. His kisses were soft and tender, infuriatingly so.

Summer felt her pussy ache, and she longed for him to touch her there. With her eyes closed she lost herself in the sensations of his touch, his kisses, his warmth. She gradually became aware of his breath becoming more rasping and his touch a little less gentle.

"I want you," he whispered.

Summer felt a gush escape her throbbing pussy. This was what she was longing for.

"I want you too," she whispered in a gasp.

She leaned back into his chest, her eyes still closed as she felt his hard, strong body next to hers.

"Lean over the desk." His whisper was husky but dominant.

Summer felt compelled to obey him. Without turning to face him, she went to the desk and braced her arms on it. She heard a slight rustle of clothing and then he was right behind her, covering her body with his as his hands curved around her and found her voluptuous breasts. She let out a sigh as he massaged the soft flesh through her dress, and she was aware that her nipples were already erect for him.

She felt one hand move from her breast and carefully unzip the back of her dress, which he slid over her shoulders in one fell swoop. She was glad she had matched her lacy underwear to her shoes and relished in the gasp of approval that escaped his lips as the dress fell to the floor.

"Very nice," he whispered close to her ear, and she felt herself flush.

His hands were back on her breasts in a second, kneading them like soft dough. He slipped the lace down, and she felt his hands on her bare skin. Her breath hitched, and she was sure she was becoming wetter again.

He caressed her and tweaked her hard nipples, sending shock waves straight to her aching pussy. Summer threw her head back as a raging inferno lit up her whole body, and she could hardly breathe for excitement.

Nathan slipped her bra off her, and then his hands went to her panties. Before removing them he rubbed the lace over her pussy, tantalizing her soaked area, and causing Summer to gasp loudly. He then pulled them down her legs.

"Keep them on," he murmured into her ear as she went to kick off her shoes.

Summer smirked, glad that she had chosen red high heels today. His hands caressed her body, and she could feel his heat. His breath was rapid in her ear, and his massive erection dug into her back.

"Bend over." His voice was deep and masterful.

With her hands still on the empty desk she bent her body over as he held a breast in each hand. Shortly afterward, one hand drifted slowly down to her pussy, and she gasped as he stroked her wet folds. A deep chuckle escaped him.

"Are you going to behave yourself now?" His words shocked her and she balked. "W-what?"

Swat! He smacked her ass, causing her to squeal as a trickle of her juice escaped down her inner thigh. God, it felt good!

"Are you going to listen to me in future?"

She wasn't sure whether he was talking about the job or just in general, but she answered straight away, "Yes, Sir."

He was rubbing away the sting in her ass now, and she longed for his fingers to return to her pussy.

"Are you going to wait for an explanation before you storm off next time?"

Summer suddenly felt indignant and hesitated. Swat!

This time the spank ricocheted through to her pussy and she gasped, afraid she was about to come on the spot.

"Yes, Sir."

"I'm glad to hear it. Now do you still want me?" His voice was like a mug of cocoa on a winter's night as he murmured softly into her ear. She loved feeling him speak to her. She had sensitive ears—a fact that Colin had exploited—but when Nathan's deep, quiet voice murmured into them, it was soothing and warm.

"Yes, Sir." She didn't hesitate.

There was a quick rustle of foil, which almost disappointed her. Nathan's passion was evident as his thick, hard cock drove into her pussy. His sigh was echoed by her gasp.

He rammed harder, and she braced herself against the polished desk. Her juices allowed him to glide effortlessly into her, and he soon became relentless as he hammered into her welcoming body.

Summer arched her back and felt the full length of him inside her. Every sweep outward touched different nerve endings, and she yelped with delight. With every thrust she could feel his massive girth and the length that seemed to go straight to her womb.

As she rose higher and higher on her cloud of ecstasy she could hear him grunting in her ear. He was as excited as she was.

Suddenly her cloud burst, stars of elation lit up her vision, and she screamed as her climax rained down. Another loud grunt later and she felt Nathan swell to mammoth proportions just before he too roared his release.

He had one hand on her hip and another on her breast as they both bent over the desk, panting hard. She could feel his heat as sweat poured from them both, mingling into a cocktail of alleviation.

After a few minutes she felt him move, and he slowly withdrew from her. Cool air surrounded her body, and she gasped at the change in sensation.

She could hear him moving around, but she was too exhausted to stir. She slumped deeper into the desk, slowly regaining her breath and her composure.

"The bathroom's through there, beautiful," he murmured, and she suddenly looked around and up into those big, warm brown eyes. He was smiling at her, stroking her hair, and she felt her breath hitch.

He really was the most handsome man in the world. She gulped as she straightened up. He had already washed and freshened up.

She nodded and picked up her clothes on her way to the small bathroom that led off from the office.

She stared at her reflection in the full-length mirror that covered the back of the door. She was wearing nothing but her red pumps, which elongated her legs, and her whole body was flushed. She looked sexy. She smiled. She *felt* sexy.

A handsome man had just taken her over the desk of his plush office. A man who actually felt something for her. She felt a burn in her stomach as she thought how much he meant to her. He was the kindest, most thoughtful man she had ever met. The fact that he was also sex on legs was a different matter entirely. God, she loved that man. Her heart filled as she thought of him. She *loved* him.

After a quick wash she felt more refreshed and got dressed. Her panties were soaked, however, and she couldn't bear the thought of having them next to her skin, so she stuffed them into her purse. Her dress was long enough to cover her modesty, and she only had to get on the bus and go home.

She cringed at the thought of going back to her apartment. Why had she been so hasty yesterday?

As she touched up her lipstick she remembered the conversation in the powder room, and her stomach churned.

"Are you OK in there?" Nathan sounded concerned as he called through, and she realized she had been longer than she intended.

"Yes, just coming," she called.

"I thought you already did that." He sniggered and she smirked, remembering the last time he had made the exact same joke. She had just started thinking of him as perfect, but his bad joke was proof that he was, in fact, human.

She emerged from his bathroom and gasped at the

sight of him in his gray suit with a clean white shirt. He had a patterned, gray tie, which complemented his look perfectly, but what really struck her was the shit-eating grin plastered all over his handsome face.

He held a hand out to her, and she slowly walked over to take it. He wrapped his arms around her and took her mouth in an earth-shattering kiss, which almost had her seeing stars again. His hot tongue explored her mouth, tentatively at first, then devoured her in his affection. Summer ran her hands through his dark waves, gently grazing her fingers on his stubble.

"Are you hungry?" he asked when he finally released his grip on her.

"I had breakfast," she told him proudly.

He chuckled. "I'm glad to hear it. Although I wasn't checking up on you. It's lunchtime. I wondered if you'd like to come eat with me. We could celebrate."

She frowned at him, a little puzzled. "Celebrate what?"

"The job, silly! You just landed yourself a job. And not just any job. You're gonna be working for the best boss in the business. Don't you feel lucky?" He grinned.

"Yeah. Cerys is lovely," she replied with a cheeky smirk.

"I didn't mean Cerys." He pouted like a child, and she couldn't help giggling. His terrible sense of humor was charming too.

"You mean I passed the induction?" she asked with a wink.

"Oh yeah, baby. You passed with flying colors." He took her in his arms again and gave her a massive hug as he nibbled at her neck.

Chapter Twelve

Summer felt his warmth and snuggled into him, caressing him lovingly.

"Is that a yes to lunch then?" he asked with a smile.

"Yes please, Sir." She looked shyly at him, and he held her even tighter before leading her out of the office.

As he opened the door she frowned. "You didn't lock the door?"

"Nope. Why would I?" He looked genuinely surprised at her concern.

"Someone might have come in."

He chuckled. "No, they wouldn't. And besides, doesn't that make it all the more exciting?"

Summer flushed as he led her to the elevator.

"Where are we going?" she asked as they got out on the ground floor.

"The restaurant. I thought you'd want to say hi to

Heaven and the others." He smiled kindly at her and her heart jolted.

"That's so thoughtful."

He smirked at her again, and she was sure he looked a little coy.

Dominic welcomed them into the restaurant and shook Nathan's hand as he led them directly to a small table in a secluded corner.

"Can't wait to have you back, Summer," he told her, making her flush.

Heaven appeared with their menus, and Summer immediately shot to her feet.

"Heaven, I'm so sorry." She felt tears threaten as she gave her friend a big hug.

"Oh, that's OK. I was worried about you in that apartment last night, though." Heaven hugged her back with a sigh.

"We all were," Nathan confided in a firm voice.

"I'm sorry. I got it all wrong." Summer shook her head as she felt herself blush.

"That's because you jumped to conclusions. It won't happen again though, will it, sugar?"

Summer's memory felt the sting on her backside again, and she shook her head. "No, Sir."

Heaven grinned and handed over the menus as Summer sat back down.

"It's leek and potato soup, and the vegetables today are julienned carrot, broccoli, and lima beans," she announced. "I'll leave you for a few minutes to choose."

"Thank you." Nathan looked very comfortable dining in the restaurant, and Summer guessed he must know all the staff.

He looked incredibly handsome in his smart suit, and his manner exactly matched that of a financial director. Summer felt a flush of pride that this gorgeous hunk was her date.

She felt a thud in her stomach as she wondered if that was all he was, though. She knew he had feelings for her—and Lord knows she had feelings for him—but had she blown her chances of a relationship after last night?

"I think I'll go for the steak, maybe shrimp to start. How about you?" He looked over his menu at her, and she felt like crying.

They were having lunch. A business lunch. At their place of work. Why would she think it was anything more? Because she had just banged the boss? Maybe that was how he recruited all his staff.

"Um...actually, I'm not hungry," she said, grabbing her purse as she felt her face begin to burn. She was about to get up when she felt his hand on her arm.

She looked up into his face. He didn't look quite so officious now, more concerned. More like the man she had been staying with these past few days.

"Talk to me, Summer. I want to know what's wrong." His voice was low and deep.

Tears pricked the edges of her eyes as she looked up into his handsome face. She felt embarrassed. She couldn't talk here; they were surrounded by people she knew. People he knew.

"I... I'm sorry about last night. I know I got it all wrong. And I'm sorry I wasn't grateful for what you did to the apartment." Her voice was not much more than a murmur, but he seemed to understand.

He shook his head and stroked her arm. "It's all right. I told you. Forget about it." He gave her a warm smile and something inside her melted.

"I am grateful. I didn't mean to hurt you," she whispered.

"I know, sugar. Why don't we forget about it and enjoy some food, huh? I'm starving. Can't think how I built up such a big appetite." He winked at her, and she giggled.

"Have you decided yet?" Heaven was back with her notepad.

"I'll have the shrimp salad and the T-bone, blue, please," Nathan told her, and Summer was grateful that he had jumped in, giving her a minute to study the menu.

"Soup and the hunter's chicken for me, please," she said with a smile.

Heaven beamed at her as she took the menus from them. "Some of the girls want to pop over and say hi, is that all right? I think they're pissed 'cause Master Dominic let me serve you today."

Summer smiled over at Nathan, awaiting his approval. He raised his eyebrows, and she nodded.

"That would be real nice," he told Heaven.

Tuesday and April suddenly appeared at the table, and Summer jumped up to hug them. It was hard to believe she had only known the girls for a few days. They had rung her and sent messages with Heaven, and had obviously been worried about her.

"When are you coming back?" April asked, excitedly.

Summer automatically looked over to Nathan for the answer.

"Soon," he told them.

"We need you back. This place is boring without you," Tuesday told them.

Summer laughed. It was good to feel so wanted.

"Nice to see you, Summer," Brad Dexter leaned in as he passed their table. She smiled at the idea of the boss's son having to be on his best behavior around her.

A look from Dominic, who stood across the room, told the girls it was time to return to work, and they quickly said their good-byes.

With new friends, a chance at a new lover, and Colin Cromer and his cronies behind bars, things were finally looking...

A thought suddenly occurred to her, and she gasped. "Nathan, there's something you should know—"

"Appetizers," Heaven announced with a smile. She placed the food on the table in front of them. "Can I get you anything else?"

"No, thank you," Nathan told her after a questioning look to Summer.

"Enjoy your meal," Heaven said brightly and left.

"Before you say anything, there's something you should know," Nathan told her, picking up a slice of his brown bread.

Summer stared up at him, her spoon in her hand.

"What we did earlier, you know it wasn't just sex, don't you?" His voice was hushed, and Summer was glad they had a secluded corner to themselves.

"What?"

"I don't do that all the time, you know," he told her with a grin. "I just wanted you to know that there was more to it than a quick session over the desk. A lot more."

Summer stared at him. He was smiling, but he looked deadly serious.

"I don't know if I'm putting this very well," he continued, looking a little embarrassed. "I just want you to know that I think you're special."

Summer gaped at him as a warm feeling flooded her bones. His hand covered hers, and he smiled.

"In fact, I think you're more than special," he continued, a little awkwardly.

She held her breath as she watched him struggle with his words. He sighed, put down his bread, and ran his hand through his hair.

"Dang it, Summer. What I'm trying to say is that I love you." He blurted the words out and then sat staring at her.

"I love you too." She didn't hesitate. She hadn't

known him long, but she knew how she felt about him. Last night proved that to her. She had missed him so badly.

He let out a relieved laugh and leaned across the table to take her mouth in a smoldering kiss. He tasted as gorgeous as he looked.

"Will you move back in with me?" He asked her tentatively. "At least until your apartment's finished?"

She felt a rush of excitement sear her bones.

"I'd love to."

He kissed her again before they resumed their meal.

"Do you always come here for your lunch?" Summer asked a little later as they began on their entrées.

Nathan sniggered. "No. I don't usually have time. However, I've heard there's this cute new waitress working here nowadays, so I might just have to get down here a little more often in future."

Summer blushed. She imagined how she would feel waiting on him, and she smiled. It would probably feel like the most natural thing in the world. She loved the idea of doing his bidding. It had worked well for her so far.

They chatted about her new role in the finance department and how many hours she could put in without exhausting herself with her restaurant duties as well.

It seemed that it would work perfectly, especially as Nathan could tailor his work to coincide with hers a lot of the time, so he would be able to drive her to and from the club. He worked a couple of nights a week as a dungeon monitor too, so that could work perfectly with her evening shifts.

"By the way, I hear a certain grocery store got shut down recently when the health inspectors called in for a surprise visit. Thought you might know it. A crummy little place on Clifford Street." Nathan dropped the little gem into conversation so casually it took her completely by surprise.

She felt her heart quicken. "Really? How did you...?"

Nathan feigned an innocent expression. "Me? Now what makes you think I had anything to do with it? I just happen to have a friend who's a lawyer, that's all." He winked at her mischievously, and she giggled.

"The guy who's helping me with the credit card scam?"

He nodded. "Yeah. He's got some friends in handy places if you know what I mean. We felt you'd been dealt a pretty shitty hand of late and thought you needed cheering up a little. Besides, we considered it our duty as upright citizens to ensure that the public was protected from out-of-date food and unsanitary conditions, you know?" He gave her a pious look as he spoke.

Summer giggled. "I'd love to have been a fly on the wall when they turned up."

"Yeah, I heard Ms. Powell wasn't too pleased. Can't imagine why. Do you want a dessert?" Nathan asked as Heaven cleared away their plates.

"No thank you, I'm full." She shook her head.

"How about coffee?" Heaven smiled.

"That would be nice," Summer replied eagerly.

"Two coffees, please," Nathan concurred, just as his cell rang. "If you'll excuse me, I'll be back in a minute," he said, getting up.

Summer smiled at him. She watched him walk out of the restaurant. He had an easy swagger that she loved. Although he was obviously very serious and professional about his work, he was also quite laid back and easygoing in his manner. She felt a warm glow knowing that he loved her. What in the world had she been so worked up about—

"Here you go," Heaven brought over the coffees with a note. "Someone from reception dropped by with a message for you too." She smiled as she gave Summer the sealed envelope.

Assuming it might be something to do with the finance job, Summer quickly opened it as Heaven went to serve coffees at another table. She was surprised to see that it was a handwritten note written on club notepaper.

Please can Summer Marsden meet Nathan Faulkner in his office right away.

Summer smirked, remembering the last time she was in his office. She also remembered that she wasn't wearing any panties. Nathan would be in for a surprise.

After taking a quick sip of her coffee, she grabbed her purse and headed joyfully for the door.

She had only got as far as the elevator when Mandy

called to her from the main entrance. "Summer. If you're looking for Master Nathan he's out here."

"Oh." A feeling of dread swept through her body. She felt her heart quicken, and she had to breathe deeply to steady her nerves.

"No, I wasn't. But thanks anyway." She tried to sound cheerful as she rushed into the elevator.

On her way up she couldn't help wondering whether Mandy had been innocent. Nathan had gone to take a call, so it was quite plausible that he might have taken it outside. But the note certainly stated he was in his office. Unless the note wasn't from him.

The elevator doors opened on the upper floor, and she got out. The other girl she had seen earlier with Mandy stood behind the reception desk, frowning at her.

Taking a deep breath, Summer strode down the corridor toward the finance office. She knew she could be walking into a trap but didn't know what else to do. She eyed everyone she saw with suspicion as she straightened her back and walked tall.

Cerys was in the main office when she arrived.

"Is Master Nathan in his office?" she blurted out as soon as she saw her.

Cerys looked surprised. "No, he told me he was going to take you to lunch."

"Listen. There's this girl called Mandy who works in HR. She and her friend who's on reception right now were talking about me in the powder room earlier, and they said that Alex Ross wants me dead. Mandy was going to speak to someone called Darren about it—isn't that the guy from the restaurant?" Summer's words tumbled out of her mouth in quick succession, while Cerys stood staring at her in amazement.

"Mandy just tried to get me to go outside. She said Nathan was out there. But I'd got this."

She showed Cerys the note. Cerys frowned.

"Who gave you this?"

"Heaven in the restaurant. I don't know who gave it to her. Someone from reception I think she said." Summer's mind raced as she tried to gather her thoughts.

"Let's find out." Cerys went into her own office.

Summer heard footsteps in the corridor and popped her head out, hoping to see Nathan coming toward her. It wasn't Nathan. It was a man she had seen before, though she couldn't recall where.

Scurrying behind him was the girl from reception with Mandy running toward them.

Summer quickly slammed the door shut and bolted it just as the guy caught up with her.

"Cerys! Get help!" she screamed as someone thumped the door.

"Get out here, whore!" She recognized his voice. He was one of Colin's friends from West Palm Beach.

"Get away from the door!" Cerys shouted, and Summer ran toward her just as a shot was fired.

"It's OK. It's bulletproof. We're finance in here, remember?" Cerys assured her as she put a comforting arm around her. "Security are on their way up. They'll have called the cops too. Come on into my room."

Summer felt her heart pound hard against her ribs as the slightly older lady led her into her small office. They could still hear shouting and thumping on the outer door, but it felt a lot safer in here.

The phone rang, and Cerys answered it immediately.

"Hi Nathan, yeah we're fine. We're holed up in here at the moment while some guy's taking potshots at the main office. I've called security. She's fine, bit shaken up, but she's OK. Want a word?"

She handed the receiver over to Summer, who was actually trembling.

"Hey, sugar, are you OK?" His voice soothed her like a warm blanket, and she instantly felt better.

"Yeah, I'm fine. I found Cerys. It's Mandy and a girl from reception. The guy's a friend of Colin's, but I don't know his name. I meant to tell you earlier but what with..."

"It's all right, baby. The cops are here now. I'll talk to you soon. You just sit tight and do whatever Cerys tells you, d'you hear?" He sounded like he had everything in hand, and Summer breathed a sigh of relief.

"Yes, Sir."

She handed the phone back to Cerys, who confirmed a couple of things with him and then placed it back down. Angry shouts could be heard, and someone thumped the door again. Summer jumped. Cerys came around the desk and put her arms around her.

"It's OK, honey. You're perfectly safe in here. The cops are here now, they'll get him."

Summer nodded, suddenly aware that tears were streaming down her cheeks. Even more shouts were heard, and then it seemed to go quiet.

"Police, open up," a man's voice called out to them as he banged on the door.

Summer jumped up in relief, but Cerys kept a hand on her shoulder.

"We don't answer it until one of the Doms... er...*management* tells us to," she told her. Summer stared at her and nodded. Her heart thumped hard in her chest, and she took a deep breath to quell the panic as she realized that she could easily have been duped.

A minute later there was a single knock on the outer door followed by three in quick succession, and then another one. Cerys smiled.

"OK, ladies, it's Nathan," came a familiar voice, and they both made their way toward the outer door.

"What's the password?" Cerys asked before unlocking the bolt.

"Lemon meringue."

She turned back to Summer with a smile. "Long story," she explained as she slid the bolt.

Slowly she opened the door a little, and then, obviously seeing her boss waiting for her, pulled it open wide.

As soon as he came into the room he gave Cerys a big hug. He looked over her shoulder and smiled at Summer, who hurriedly wiped the tears from her face.

Nathan loosened his grip on Cerys, and Brad came to take his place, holding her even tighter than Nathan had. Brad took her through to her own little office, affording Cerys some privacy.

Nathan immediately put his arms around Summer, wrapping her in a cloak of security and affection.

She clung to him as uncontrollable tears flooded her face. He enveloped her in his strength, and she breathed him into her soul.

"I'm so proud of you, sugar," he whispered into her ear. "You did everything right."

"Sh-she said you were outside. I didn't trust her, not after..."

"It's all right. You did exactly the right thing. This has to be the safest part of the whole building. You did right to come up here. And Cerys knows all the protocols for a security breach. You couldn't have been in better hands. Well, other than mine, of course." He chuckled and she couldn't help smiling.

Nathan held her until she stopped shaking and everyone had left, then sat her down. He picked up her purse from the desk where she had left it and opened it.

"I'll just get you a Kleenex. I presume there's one in..." His voice trailed off as his hand brought out a scrap of red material that he had obviously assumed was her handkerchief.

Chapter Thirteen

Summer blushed with horror. Nathan's lips turned up into a salacious grin, and he cocked one eyebrow. He looked so sexy, Summer gasped. He dangled the panties on one finger and looked questioningly at her.

"I... er... well, you see, after we... um... " she stammered, but couldn't make a coherent sentence to save her life right at that minute.

She felt herself go hot all over, and she felt an ache in her pussy, much like the one she had experienced earlier. She squeezed her thighs together, thankful that she was sitting down.

"Tell me again why you came up here," he said slowly.

"The note said you wanted to see me in your office. I thought..."

"You thought *what*, exactly?"

"I thought you might be up here. Well, at first I did. I thought you might want to... you know... like we did earlier. Then Mandy was in the foyer saying that you were outside. I meant to tell you about what I heard her say in the ladies' room earlier—that Alex Ross wanted me dead."

Nathan's face clouded over. "When did she say that?"

Summer swallowed hard. "It was when I first arrived. Before my interview. I was going to tell you when I saw you, but then Cerys interviewed me and then you...er...it went right out of my head."

He frowned. "So why didn't you tell me at lunch?"

"I was going to but you said...well, you said..." Her voice dwindled off as he took a step closer.

"I said I love you."

She nodded. "And I couldn't think of anything else."

He sat on the edge of the desk, and his lips enveloped hers. It was a sweet kiss, lingering and slow.

"I'm sorry. I should have listened to you. You said you had something to tell me, and I thought it might be something I didn't want to hear. I needed to tell you how I felt before you made any decisions." His voice was quiet.

"Decisions about what?"

He sighed. "I was afraid you might be about to tell me that you didn't want to see me anymore because of what I did to your apartment. I needed to let you know that the reason I did it all was because I love you. I wanted to keep you safe." He bit his lip.

Summer stood slowly and held his face in her hands. She kissed him slowly and lovingly, savoring every second.

His hands ran down her body, stopping at her curved ass. A low chuckle resounded through his chest as he lingered on the area, covered only by the thin material of her dress.

"I think I'll make this part of your uniform," he murmured. "No panties in the office. Yeah, I like the sound of that."

Summer giggled, pulling back from the kiss to hug him tight.

There was a knock at the open door, and they both jumped around to see Steve Ratner standing there with a grin on his face.

"Just a few questions if you've got the time."

"Make it quick," Nathan growled, stuffing the panties into his pocket.

Ratner guffawed and whipped out his notebook. "Cerys has told me what happened after you got in here. Good move, by the way. How did you come to be upstairs though? Weren't you in the restaurant?" He stared at Summer, still safely ensconced in her lover's arms.

"Heaven gave me this. I think it was from reception," Summer explained, handing over the note. She went on to tell him all about Mandy and the other girl, the conversation in the powder room, and how Mandy had tried to lure her outside.

"Damn good job you had the sense not to go with her," Steve said with a serious frown. "You could have ended up anywhere, and we'd have no way of knowing."

Summer felt Nathan hold her a little tighter as the realization hit them all.

"I didn't trust her. Then I didn't know if I was being fooled by the note. Nathan wasn't here, so I guess someone was just playing a trick there." Summer frowned thoughtfully. "I wonder who sent the note."

"The same person who sent me the prank call, I guess," Nathan said, handing his cell over to Ratner.

"Hmm, did they speak to you?"

"Yeah. It was a guy. Vaguely familiar, I think, but I'm not certain. It was a bad reception, so I took it in one of the offices downstairs." Nathan pouted, obviously quite pissed at being duped.

"Did anyone see you take the call?" Steve asked, narrowing his eyes.

Nathan's eyes widened. "Yeah. Mandy from HR was hanging around the foyer when I went through. I didn't think anything of it."

"OK, we'll look into it. I'll let you know as soon as I find out anything. In the meantime, enjoy your afternoon." Steve gave Nathan a knowing wink and put his notebook back into his pocket. He saluted Summer before leaving.

No sooner had he left the room than Brad and Cerys came in. Nathan huffed.

"Take the rest of the day off, Cerys. You did great today," he told her.

"Thanks." Cerys grinned.

"I'll take you home," Brad offered as she went back into her office and grabbed her purse.

"Come on, let's get out of here, too," Nathan murmured as soon as they'd left the room.

Summer giggled as he led her out of the office and carefully locked the door behind them.

They sped off, but didn't go straight back to Nathan's house as she had expected. Instead they veered off and went up a country lane.

"It's no good. I can't wait any longer," he said, pulling up in a secluded spot by some trees. "The thought of you sitting there with no panties on is driving me wild."

He took her hand and led her over to a large tree, where he pinned her against the soft bark. Taking her mouth in a hard kiss, she heard him moan and felt herself weaken in his hold.

Surrounded by him, she could only surrender to his masculinity and melt in his embrace. Nathan took both of her arms and held them in one of his large hands above her head.

Summer felt her breasts thrust toward him, and he devoured them through the fabric of her shift dress. His breath was hot, and his tongue drenched her as he deliciously teased her sensitive nipples to two hard nubs of pure sensation.

She gasped as she felt his other hand trail down to the hem of her dress, hitching it up to her waist. The cool afternoon air wafted around her damp pussy, and she had never felt so wanton.

Pressing her mound against his rock-hard erection, she moaned as her breathing became more erratic and her passion accelerated.

Suddenly she heard the sound of his zipper being unfastened and felt his velvet skin nudge her outer labial lips. Her breath hitched, and she could feel his ardor as he clamped her to the tree trunk with his whole body while his leg came between hers, forcing them wider apart.

With his one free hand he pulled a foil wrapper from his pocket and tore it open with his teeth. As soon as he was sheathed she felt his finger dip into her juices, gently grazing her clit, before lubricating the rubber.

Summer felt a burn deep inside her stomach, and she licked and kissed his neck as he lined himself up against her.

"Tell me you want me, sugar." His rasping voice hissed desperately, and she could feel the tension in his body as he restrained himself.

"I want you," she assured him.

That was enough. With one deep thrust he was inside her, pushing his massive length right up her soaking channel, reawakening the nerves that danced for joy as they worshipped his manhood.

Summer couldn't resist pressing herself against him,

eliciting every last sensation from their conjoined bodies. The inferno inside her swept through her bones, and she felt herself tremble with excitement as she reached her peak.

Screaming his name, she clung to him for dear life as wave upon wave of ecstasy consumed her body and soul.

She was rewarded by his guttural grunt as he released his boiling cream into the pocket of rubber, which deprived her once again of his seed. In that second she felt that she was handing herself over to him, completely and unconditionally, and she felt his hold on her even stronger than ever.

They slumped against each other, panting for air, unable to speak, hardly capable of coherent thought as their sated bodies gradually returned to earth.

"I love you," she whispered at last.

Nathan's gorgeous face pulled back from hers slightly, his eyes still black with desire. A light sheen glowed across his skin, and his breath was still rasping a little as he gave her a sultry grin.

"I love you, sugar," he told her, staring into her eyes. His lips encased hers once more as he took her in a languid, sensual kiss, which had her gasping for breath.

"Let's go fetch your things," he said with a wink when they finally composed themselves and headed back to the car.

"There's nothing I'd like more," she assured him.

It didn't take long to get back to the apartment and

gather her belongings, as most of it was still packed from last night.

On their way out of the house Nathan set the intruder alarm.

Summer frowned. "I don't understand why you had that installed when you wanted me to come stay with you anyway," she commented.

Nathan looked surprised. "I know you. You're an independent woman. You might not have wanted to live with me. I wouldn't take a thing like that for granted," he told her.

Summer thought about it as they sped off to his place. She was glad he felt that way. He was her Dom and knew what was best for her, but he wasn't going to try to take over her life. She was pleased that she was still able to make her own decisions.

She snuggled into him as he drove down the freeway. Every minute she spent with him she seemed to fall in love with him a little more.

It was a delight to put her things away in the closet and bathroom of his master bedroom. Where they belonged, she thought. She went back into the lounge to hear Nathan speaking on the phone. He beckoned to her to sit beside him on the couch while he listened to the caller. He frowned.

"OK, buddy, thanks for letting me know." He finished up, replacing the receiver.

She looked up at him questioningly.

"That was Steve Ratner. It seems Mandy Burrage

finally came clean about what she's been up to. She's had a relationship going with Darren Hall who, incidentally, she moved in with recently. She managed to keep it under the radar because he works for us too, so it wasn't actually picked up as a new address. Also, working in HR meant she was better able to hide the fact. She was also two-timing Hall by seeing that guy who showed up at the club today. I knew I recognized the voice on the phone."

Summer frowned. "Darren Hall? Isn't that the sommelier?"

"Sure is. The guy Dominic suspected of getting another job. Well, he sure did. He was working for Alex Ross. That's why he was seen in a bar across town. He wasn't serving wine though. He was dealing drugs." Nathan was visibly seething.

"Darren? Oh my God!" Summer's jaw almost hit the ground. She hadn't actually met him, as he hadn't been in to work since she started, but she'd heard a lot about him.

Nathan held her a little closer. "The big guy at the club was called Hayden Monk. He also worked for Ross. Do you know him?"

Summer's eyes widened, and she felt herself go hot.

"Of course—Monkey! He was a friend of Colin's back in West Palm Beach. I knew I'd seen him before."

"Well, it turns out that Mandy was sleeping with both him and Hall. She had told Monk about this new girl at the club—just pillow talk, you know—and Monk mentioned it to Ross.

"Cromer had already told Ross that you'd fled the area, so he had his ear to the ground and managed to add two and two.

"Hall was just small fry, but Ratner's dead chuffed to have picked up Monk at long last. They've been trying to get him for a while, but he keeps moving up and down the coast whenever anyone gets close. He's quite a brutal bastard by all accounts."

Summer shuddered. Looked like another lucky escape.

"So how come your spies didn't know that Mandy was seeing Monk or that Darren was involved with Alex Ross and his gang? I thought they knew everything." She frowned. "And another thing. Why did Mandy send that note telling me to meet you in the office and then say you were outside instead?"

"The note was from the receptionist, Sandra. She and Mandy got their wires crossed. A last-minute change in the plan that didn't get passed on. And Mandy did a good job keeping quiet about Monk because she didn't want Hall finding out she was cheating on him.

"We knew Hall was up to something, but no one suspected him of getting into anything as big as this. He hasn't worked at the club for long, and most of the time he's been on the payroll he's been off work, supposedly sick.

"We hadn't got much on him yet, but we were working on it. That's how we came to find out he was in that dang bar downtown. Turns out he'd only just got involved with the gang in the last few days, anyhow."

Nathan looked frustrated that they hadn't got the intel on him sooner.

"Unlucky for him," Summer said, pursing her lips thoughtfully.

Nathan must have caught her uneasy expression.

"Still want to work at Collar and Cuffs?"

She looked up into his gorgeous face and smiled.

"Definitely. Seems like the safest place on earth."

Nathan kissed her cheek with a smile. "I'm glad you said that, sugar. It seems like we're going to be keeping you mighty busy over there for a while. What with the finance job, waiting on, and now a sommelier's position to fill, I reckon you're gonna be rushed off your feet from now on."

"It's not my feet I'm worried about," she told him with a salacious wink.

The End

Waiting On Tuesday

COLLAR AND CUFFS BOOK 2 - BONUS
MATERIAL

"What in heaven's name did you do that fer?" Tuesday O'Leary's broad Irish accent resounded around the busy restaurant of Collar and Cuffs, and all eyes looked disparagingly toward table twenty-three. Tutting, she took her serving cloth from the top of the dumbwaiter and went over to wipe up the spilled gravy as an elderly gentleman stood up slowly, his chair gouging a deep path through the plush carpet.

"It was an accident. I knocked it," he murmured, turning a bright shade of scarlet before scurrying off toward the men's room to clean himself up.

"Is there a problem here?" The calm, commanding voice of Dominic Ray, the handsome Maitre d', could be heard subtly checking on the waitress, who shook her head sulkily.

"Good. Then I suggest you rectify this mess quickly and get on with serving table twenty-one. They're waiting for the dessert menu." His crisp, no-nonsense tone indicated to the watching diners the situation was resolved, and the murmur of polite conversation soon resumed.

As soon as the boss's back was turned, Tuesday rolled her eyes, swiftly cleared up the spill, and took the now-empty gravy boat to the kitchen for a refill.

Dominic threw her a warning look when she re-emerged, and she plastered on her best fake smile as she returned to the table and served her customers.

Tuesday's attempts to hide her irritation failed miserably, and when the customer from table twenty-nine got up to leave and knocked into the table, causing two crystal wineglasses to smash onto the floor, she'd had just about had enough.

"Holy Mother of God! Watch what you're doing, can't you?" she hollered, pulling a chair out of the way and crawling on the floor to collect up the larger pieces of shattered glass.

Dominic was there in a flash. "Tuesday, leave that and take five," he ordered in a clipped tone.

She felt herself go hot and her face flushed. His expression told her not to argue, and she reluctantly placed the broken glass on the table before leaving the room. She could feel everyone's eyes on her as she made her way toward the large rest area.

Dominic's steady tone, as he pacified the customers and ordered Summer and Hope to deal with the mess, rankled, and she couldn't wait to be out of there.

She slumped heavily into a soft chair at the opposite end of the room from the lockers and wiped her face as hot, angry tears started to swamp her cheeks. It was all too much.

After a few minutes she felt a little better and went over to wash her face.

She checked the time. Not long before the shift ended. Good. She sighed, relishing the thought of going downstairs to the dungeon. She wanted a good, heavy session tonight. Maybe over the spanking bench, or, better still, the St. Andrew's cross. She didn't even mind if the Dom used a crop after the day she'd just had—she'd welcome the bite on her tensed-up body.

"Are you OK?" Heaven had come to find her. Here would be the voice of reason. Heaven always managed to maintain a clear head in a crisis, and the girls loved her for it. Heck, the men loved her for it too. There wasn't a person in the building who didn't love Heaven Blake.

Tuesday took a paper towel and wiped over her face, smudging her mascara.

"Yeah, I just got a bit sick of those clumsy eedjits, that's all." She forced herself to smile at her friend, who gave her a friendly hug.

"We all get days like that," Heaven assured her. "I think most of the time the punters have had too much to drink, though they'd never admit it." She chuckled.

"I know the guy with the gravy had—stank of whiskey, he did. Damn well deserved to go home with a wet patch on his pants." Tuesday thought back to the old man and giggled.

Heaven hugged her a little tighter and laughed too. "They always get their comeuppance, I'm sure of it," she agreed.

Tuesday took a deep breath. "Well, back to the grind, I suppose."

"If you're sure you're OK?" Heaven smiled at her sympathetically.

"Oh, I'm all right. Don't you be worrying about me," Tuesday assured her with a nod.

Heaven linked her arm and Tuesday led the way back to the restaurant. Dominic nodded at them as they walked in, and Heaven gave her another quick hug before going back to her own station.

Tuesday was relieved to see that most of her customers had now left for the night, and Summer was busy re-laying table twenty-three.

"Thanks," she whispered, going over to help.

"That's OK. Are you all right?" Summer whispered with a kind smile.

"I'm grand." Tuesday managed a grin, and Summer gave her a quick hug before finishing off the table.

Tuesday went over to serve desserts to table twenty-four, the last of her deuces, before her large party on twenty-seven got up to leave.

"Don't worry about relaying that one," Dominic murmured in her ear as she began to clear it. "Just leave it tidy and it can wait until tomorrow."

Tuesday nodded gratefully. She stacked everything up neatly to show how much she appreciated his kindness. The other bosses she'd had over the years wouldn't have been so forgiving.

She was relieved when it was time for the curtain call and strolled over to where the rest of the waiting on staff were congregating, ready for Dominic's round up of the night's service before they would all be dismissed.

"Well done, everyone. Another very busy service, but you managed to keep your heads and not bite off too many of the customers'." He stared pointedly at Tuesday and everyone giggled.

Tuesday wasn't surprised when he ended his little speech with, "Tuesday, a word before you go, please."

She watched everyone else leave the room and took a deep breath. Always in the shit, she told herself, it was only the depth that varied. Somehow she always seemed to attract trouble for one reason or another.

Dominic peered at her as if he was looking at her very soul. She was accustomed to this type of scrutiny from the Doms of Collar and Cuffs. She often wondered what they could see that no one else could. "Is everything all right?" he asked eventually.

Tuesday nodded. "Everything's just hunky-dory, boss. Just had a handful of careless punters tonight, that's all." She shrugged.

He frowned. "Are you sure that's all it is?"

"Yes, Sir." She didn't dare look into those gorgeous dark eyes of his.

"OK. Well, get some rest and I'll see you tomorrow."

She could tell that he wasn't convinced, but there was no way she was going to spill her life story. And certainly not to a Dom.

She nodded politely and got out of there as quickly as she could.

Everyone had left the changing room by the time she got there, and she was glad not to have to speak to anyone. She quickly undressed and had a wash before pulling on a short skirt and a bandeau top. She didn't bother with shoes, and relished the feel of the cold floor on her bare feet.

She had worked at Collar and Cuffs long enough to get used to waiting on in the customary high heels, but she always loved the feeling of comfort when she took them off.

She took the elevator to the lower ground floor and enjoyed the sensation of relief when the doors opened just outside the dungeon.

The heavy throb of the music pulsated through her brain, drowning out the nagging thoughts and worries hidden there.

Tuesday lowered her eyes as Roland Dexter, the club owner, passed her on her way into the Bottom Bar, but she quickly looked up again when she heard voices near the door.

"Good evening, Tuesday." She'd know that deep tone anywhere. It's what attracted her to the place more than anything else, though she'd never admit it.

"Master Dan. How the devil are ya?" She grinned cheekily at the handsome man, and he shook his head wearily. She could tell his stress didn't come entirely from her impertinent behavior. Perhaps they could help each other blow off some steam...

"Is that really how you address a Dom?" His deep blue eyes bore into her.

"After the day I've had it is, sure enough," she replied, staring defiantly at him.

An excited rush swept through her, and she watched him deciding whether or not to give her what he felt she needed— what she really wanted.

"I can sure see why you were just one warning away from being dismissed early last week. Are you here to play tonight, sub?" His voice was deep and masterful, and filled her with hope.

"I am, Sir. Are you?"

She saw his jaw tense at her response, and could tell he was considering his options. She knew she was playing with fire, acting up when she could so easily be thrown out of the club altogether, but she trusted Master Dan to sense her need.

"Not really. I'm trying to figure a way to vet all of these new members the boss has invited to the club, but I can see that will have to wait. You, little one, need to be reminded how to behave when you're addressing a Dom."

She tried to quell her excitement and rolled her eyes

heavenward in an attempt to re-affirm that she did, indeed, need to be taught a lesson.

With a sigh, Master Dan took her by the arm and led her over to the St. Andrew's cross.

Tuesday didn't need any instruction. She climbed straight up and positioned herself while he secured her wrists and ankles to the smooth wooden structure. She let out a silent exhale of relief as she allowed herself to sink into the wood.

"I don't know what the problem is with you, Tuesday O'Leary," Master Dan was saying sternly. "You have been here long enough to know the correct way to act. Is there any reason why you choose not to behave properly in the club?"

"No, Sir." She lied.

She heard him sigh again.

"Then maybe a little punishment might remind you of what is expected here."

She had her back to him, and heard a little reluctance in his voice. Like any good Dom, he was attentive to her needs, and she knew he'd always want to make sure he would be inflicting more pleasure than pain.

Soon she heard the sound of the single-tail being whipped through the air a couple of times before it landed with a thwack on her back.

She welcomed its sting like a long-lost friend and sank deeper into the wood beneath her, without a sound.

The next hit was slightly harder, followed by another and then another.

Tuesday closed her eyes, welcoming the physical pain on her back which temporarily suffocated the mental pain in her heart.

She couldn't get enough of it and relished every stroke.

As the leather came crashing onto her skin she imagined it was drowning out the shouting in her head.

The force of each sweep pushed away the memories that haunted her, banishing them to the far corners of her mind which even she couldn't reach.

Each stroke on her back was another recollection, another fear, being driven out of her mind and vanquished to kingdom come. She knew they would be back to taunt her before too long, but for now they were gone. Gone, just like…

"Your color, Tuesday. I asked for your color, little one." Master Dan's gentle voice wafted into her mind, pulling her back toward reality. She slowly opened her eyes and was shocked at how blurry everything was. She had been crying.

"Come on, that's enough for tonight." His deep, calm voice washed over her as his large hands unfastened her from the cross and he carefully lifted her down.

She felt a burn in her stomach; she wasn't ready to face reality again just yet.

"Master Dan, I need… I want…" she whispered, staring into his deep blue eyes.

He looked at her a little surprised, raising one eyebrow in question.

"Little one, I don't think you're in any fit state to..."

"Please, Master Dan. Please, I need this. I need you," she pleaded.

Master Dan stopped on his way to the sofas.

"Tuesday, do you want to talk?"

She shook her head. Talking was the last thing she wanted to do.

He hesitated.

"Please, Master Dan. I really want to."

"We'll take it slowly," he said as he turned and carried her down the hall and past the playrooms.

He found a bedroom and took her in. It was warm, dimly lit, and smelled of sandalwood.

She felt the soft bed beneath her as he gently laid her down, and felt bereft the second his arms let her go.

She reached up for him, desperate to feel his skin against hers again.

"I hope you're not thinking of topping from the bottom," he warned.

Quickly she withdrew her hand from his shoulder, terrified he would change his mind.

He didn't.

She watched him slowly remove his shirt, his bare chest heaving as his arms rippled. He was looking at her the whole time, studying her reaction.

Tuesday knew he wouldn't take advantage of a sub, even one as desperate as she.

She bit her lip as she felt a gush from her pussy.

As his pants fell to the floor his erection was evident through his black Calvin Klein's.

She licked her lips as he removed them, staring at him as he bent over her.

"Your turn." His big hands were gentle as he reached down and removed her skimpy top.

Her breasts flopped free, nipples tight. She trembled with anticipation.

He didn't disappoint. His confident fingers slipped her tiny skirt down her legs, before he ran a warm hand over her soaking mound.

With a grin he pulled off her sodden panties, and she gasped as the air touched her over-sensitized skin.

She looked up at his shining, blue eyes, feeling her heart thump heavily as she panted for breath.

Pleading silently, she willed him to take her.

His hand stroked her pussy as his mouth smothered hers, and the bed dipped as he elegantly climbed over her. She gasped as his long fingers slipped into her, and her stomach burned with excitement.

"You're ready for me, little one," he murmured.

"Yes."

Tuesday knew he would only do this if he was sure it was what she wanted. He had taken her before, once with Master Nathan, and once on his own. She knew he was a generous lover, and that was what she needed right now. She needed him.

His engorged, sheathed cock nudged gently at her dripping entrance before plunging deep into her. She was conscious of him continually watching her expression, and she gasped as his massive member stretched her deliciously.

After giving them both a minute to adjust, he began pumping, gently at first, and then harder.

Tuesday gazed up at the gorgeous hunk, marveling at his ability to take her so fully, while keeping his weight off of her.

His muscles rippled and his eyes shone as he heaved his massive cock in and out, his breathing becoming more rapid and beads of sweat rolling down his chest.

She closed her eyes briefly, exalting in the feeling of utter abandon. The fire inside her roared and her pussy clenched. She was floating on air, soaring higher and higher with every thrust.

"Look at me, little one." His voice was gentle in its command.

Her eyes sprang open and she stared into his beautiful face. His expression took her breath away. He was excited, as desperate as she was for their inevitable release.

"Tell me when," he murmured.

The realization of what he meant ratcheted her feelings up the final notch.

"Now, now, Master Dan!"

She felt her orgasm gush through her like a waterfall, soaring to the moon before exploding as a million stars danced in front of her eyes. She heard his roar as he released his load at the same time, and in that instant she hated the small film of rubber which denied her his seed.

Again and again she came, his moans egging her on as he continued to plough into her eager body, fulfilling her aching need.

Eventually she felt his cock soften inside her and she slowly began her descent back to earth. He moved to her side, and she snuggled into his touch.

Every inch of her body needed to be in contact with his. She wanted to be inside his skin.

He held her tightly as they both heaved for the same air.

Tuesday felt herself sinking as the euphoria gradually left her and the real world beckoned her once again. For a few minutes she just lay in his warm arms, slowly taking it all in.

She recalled that she was here, in the dungeon of Collar and Cuffs, her favorite place in the whole world. Master Dan was whispering quietly to her, urging her to close her eyes. She felt her lids become heavy and momentarily shut them, feeling drowsy and relaxed.

Like a knife cutting into her, realization suddenly took its grip and she sat up, wide-eyed.

"Shh, it's all right, little one. Just relax. Everything's all right." Master Dan was trying to pull her back into his embrace, but she knew better than to let him.

"No, really, I'm fine now. I have to be getting back. Thanks all the same."

He frowned at her as she pushed him away and leaped to her feet, yanking on her clothes as she went.

She literally ran out of the dungeon and into the

elevator. She had left her things in the changing room by the restaurant, not the one down here.

As she pressed the button for the upper floor, she saw Master Dan rushing toward her in just his trousers.

Luckily the doors closed in time, and she heaved a sigh of relief as she made her way up without him.

She knew there was a good chance he would be waiting for her in the ground floor reception area once she was ready to go home, but was glad that at least she had had time to gather her thoughts and compose herself before she saw him again.

When she came back, she saw he'd pinned himself to the front entrance. Smart.

"Tuesday, we need to talk." His authoritative tone made her clench her pussy with excitement, but she didn't have time to savor the moment right now. It was a pity. Even fully dressed he looked as delectable as ever.

"I'm sorry, Sir. I have to catch my bus."

She tried to barge past him, but he grabbed her arms firmly.

"Why won't you speak to me?"

She stared into his gorgeous face. His big blue eyes were pleading with her, his beautiful blond hair shining in the fluorescent lighting of the reception area.

She felt a jolt inside of her. He would be so easy to talk to. He might even make her forget, just for a while. He had just cleansed her mind; perhaps he could cleanse her soul too. But at what cost? What could she give him in return? Her misery, her suffering? Her past was a torrid mixture of pain and fear, her present made up of anguish and heartache, and her future... what future? No. She had nothing to offer him or anyone else. She shook her head.

"Let me drive you home." He looked sad, troubled.

"No, thank you. I really have to go."

She broke free from his grip, and he let her leave. She knew he didn't want to. But he was a Dom. He knew when no meant no. The cold night enveloped her, and she took a deep breath, welcoming its sharp chill.

She had changed into her jeans and sneakers for the journey home, and quickly made her way around the corner to the bus stop.

While she waited the ten minutes or so for the bus, she felt that she was being watched. Not in a sinister way. More, being watched *over*. Looked out for.

She smiled to herself, guessing Master Dan wouldn't be far away. Such a kind man and a good friend. He had given her what she asked for, and she felt guilty that she couldn't do the same for him.

She could never allow anyone in on her secrets though. Secrets that were a part of her life in a way, sadly, Master Dan would never be.

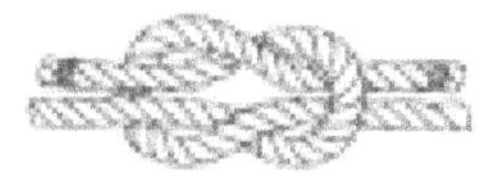

May I ask a favor?

I really hope you enjoyed reading Waiting On Summer. If so, I'd love it if you could leave a review (one or two words is fine) at any of the following:

Goodreads

Bookbub

Thank you so much

dangerous boyfriend, Carla Burchfield falls in love with hunky twin cowboys, Matt and Dyson Shearer.

When Pearson turns up in town Carla's first instinct is to flee. Reluctantly leaving the guys, she makes her escape, only to be met with an accident en route. Local rancher, Aiden Fielding finds her and takes her back to his palatial spread, where he calls the doctor and the sheriff's office. To Carla's horror she discovers that the local Deputy Sheriff is, in fact, Dyson Shearer.

Feeling upset and betrayed she flees the ranch, taking with her a broken heart and a head full of secrets the guys would never believe.

When Pearson catches up with her, so does her past. Can she ever convince her cowboys that her reasons for hiding the stolen cash from a shop-raid are actually honorable? And can they persuade her to stay with them even though the affluent Aiden Fielding appears to have so much more to offer her?

The Cowboys of Cavern County Series
Carla's Cowboys (Book One)
Maggie's Man (Book Two)
Two for Trinity (Book Three)
Isla's Irish Cowboy (Book Four)
Savannah's Saviors (Book Five)
Rihanna's Rancher (Book Six)

Your Next Read:

The *Collar and Cuffs* Series
Waiting on Tuesday (Book Two)

Nathan is around to rescue her. I'm now looking forward to reading all the other books written by this author. Great read and entertaining, didn't want to put it down, however I HAD TO at times!! Thanks Bella!!

5 STARS

About the Author

Bella Settarra began writing for a living after having to give up her full-time job due to the after-effects of breast cancer. She has always had a positive outlook and saw this as an opportunity to do what she really wanted to do with her life—write.

She has always enjoyed writing but had never actually submitted anything for publication before. After undergoing a rather gruelling and depressing medical procedure, her husband promised to take her to a reader-writer event, which is where she met lots of authors who encouraged her to try writing for a publisher.

The event, aptly named *Smut by the Sea* was mainly for authors of Erotic Romance and Erotica, something Bella had never contemplated writing before. However, on the long journey home she started to write a short story which grew into a novella.

An author-friend offered to critique the first chapter for her and told her to send it to a publisher as she thought it was really good. The book was accepted shortly after and *Last of the Sirens* became the first of a series of six!

After that series, *Sirens and Sailors*, she went on to

write Cowboy Romances, which she loves. She currently has three cowboy series, *The Men of Moone Mountain*, *The Cowboys of Cavern County*, and the more conventional *Midnight in Montana*.

Although still writing her cowboy stories, she wanted to write a story about people who work in a restaurant, which is a subject close to her heart.

When she was younger, Bella wanted to go to away to University to study English in order to become a writer, but was told she couldn't go, so was persuaded to go to the local Catering College instead. Although she didn't much enjoy cooking, she loved working in the restaurant and went on to get several waiting on jobs before running a restaurant herself. She loved the camaraderie of the staff, and the "pomp and circumstance" of waiting on.

She has finally combined both her loves by writing this series, *Collar and Cuffs*, which follows the staff working in the restaurant of a swanky BDSM club—sex and food, what more can you ask for? LOL ;)

She hopes you enjoy reading her stories as much as she enjoys writing them. Feel free to sign up to her Newsletter and connect with her at any of the following:

Facebook

Twitter

Instagram

Goodreads

Bookbub

Newsletter

Check out her website